38

3 1780 00031 4807

DATE DUE

JUN 0 6 2006

Westville Public Library
Westville IL. 61883

DEMCO

Westville Public Library
Westville, IL 61883

GARNET

Other books by Carolyn Brown:

The *Promised Land Romance* Series:
Willow
Velvet
Gypsy

The *Land Rush Romance* Series:
Emma's Folly
Violet's Wish
Maggie's Mistake
Just Grace

Love Is
A Falling Star
All the Way from Texas
The Yard Rose
The Ivy Tree
Lily's White Lace
That Way Again

GARNET

•

Carolyn Brown

AVALON BOOKS
NEW YORK

© Copyright 2004 by Carolyn Brown
Library of Congress Catalog Card Number: 2004090294
ISBN 0-8034-9666-4
All rights reserved.
All the characters in this book are fictitious,
and any resemblance to actual persons,
living or dead, is purely coincidental.
Published by Thomas Bouregy & Co., Inc.
160 Madison Avenue, New York, NY 10016

PRINTED IN THE UNITED STATES OF AMERICA
ON ACID-FREE PAPER
BY HADDON CRAFTSMEN, BLOOMSBURG, PENNSYLVANIA

With love to
Lilybet Rhian Harmon;
our newest addition to the family.

Chapter One

Garnet Diana Dulan swung open the doors of the Silver Dollar Saloon, sucked up a lung full of cigar smoke, listened intently to the sounds of men playing poker and the scrape of boots across the wooden floor and felt right at home. One minute inside the doors and she knew she'd made the right decision to leave the wagon train. Two minutes inside the swinging doors and everything in the saloon went stone cold silent. What was a decent woman doing inside a saloon? She had to be someone's irate wife or one of those temperance ladies. Either one would ruin the whole evening.

Garnet strolled over to the bar, propped one dusty, worn boot up on the railing around the bottom and eyed the barkeep. "Pour me up a double shot of your cheapest whiskey," she said, careful to keep her ankles covered beneath the full-skirted, cotton dress faded to a nondescript shade of blue from months of walking beside a wagon train twelve hours a day in the broiling sun.

"Lady, I don't serve decent women in this place. If you're lookin' for a fight with your husband, then just pick out the sorry scoundrel and drag him home by the ear. If you're one of them temperance women and you're here to throw that whiskey back in my face, then just take your

views right on back out that door. I don't want no trouble,
no matter who you are." The barkeep eyed her seriously,
one heavy dark eyebrow rising slightly as he did so. She
was a lovely lady, all right. A full head of deep red hair
she'd pulled back into a bun at the nape of her slender
neck. The strangest colored blue eyes, big and round and
staring at him with a hint of humor in them. And a face
carved from pure porcelain, reminding him of the figurine
his mother had always kept on the mantel above the fireplace in Kentucky.

"I'm neither one, Mister," Garnet said, a touch of Southern grace coating her words. "I'm a saloon piano player
and I need a job. I'll play tonight for the price of a double
shot of whiskey to sit on my piano for the evening. If you
like my style, you can hire me and we'll negotiate for the
job. I'll require a room and board. Suppose you got both?"

"Lady, I don't need a piano player," the barkeep rolled
his dark eyes toward the ceiling.

"Well, you got one for this evening. Room and board
and we'll talk about the rest later," Garnet said. "Pour me
up a whiskey and if you don't like my style or how many
men a tinkling piano can drag in here off the streets, then
I'll go on my way after tonight. You got nothing to lose
but a double shot of whiskey."

"Why the whiskey?" he asked, already pouring it into a
sparkling clean glass.

"I set it on the top of that piano," she nodded toward the
polished upright piano in the corner. "Then when the men
start coming by to ask to buy me a drink, I just nod at it.
That way I'm not beholden to anyone for buying a drink.
I never drink the vile stuff or any other liquor. But rest
assured, I'm not of the temperance movement either. Per-
sonally, I'm a sweet tea drinker of the evenings, just like
you are." She cut her eyes to the glass on the bar. "On a
morning which starts about noon, I like coffee, dark as
black strap molasses. I'm not temperance and I'm nobody's

wife. I played the Lucky Lady in Little Rock, Arkansas for two years, so I know what I'm doing."

"Then give it your best shot, Miss Dulan. I'm not going to hire you but if you've a mind to play all evening for a shot of whiskey that you don't plan to drink, then just get after it," the barkeep said. "I'm Jonah. Those four girls over there are here to keep the men's glasses full. They've got rooms upstairs. If you did happen to work out, which you won't, there'd be an extra one for you. I don't hire women like you. If I want a piano player, I'm inclined to be interested in a man to play, not a woman in a calico dress and her hair done up in a bun like someone's old maid aunty. And by the way, if I had a change of heart and did hire you, there's no men allowed upstairs. Woman wants to do that kind of work, they can go down to Jezebel's Parlor."

Garnet nodded, carried the glass of the foul smelling amber liquid to the piano, set it on the top and pulled out the bench. She stretched her fingers and hit the keys running with a livened-up rendition of "Yellow Rose of Texas" followed by a fast version of the "Jenny Lind Polka." By the time she'd finished that, she'd already turned down three offers for a drink. Men were straggling in from outside to lean against the bar, tap their feet in time to the music, and the four barmaids were having trouble keeping up with the orders.

A wide grin split Jonah's face, and the other girls began to eye the prim and proper lady at the piano with jealousy. She looked more like a schoolmarm than she did a saloon piano player, but the place, usually dead by that time of night, was jumping with business. They'd already served more men than they usually did in a whole week, so even if they didn't like the new lady, they sure did appreciate the way she could make that piano do everything but stand up and talk.

Garnet had just finished "Dixie," a brand new song she'd just learned the year before, when she looked up into the bluest eyes she'd ever seen. The man was leaning on the edge of the piano, so close to the glass of whiskey that his nose twitched at the cheapness of it. His face was a study in angles with a strong chin, the slightest of clefts in the middle. Not a smooth chin. Not cut with a deep cleft. Just enough to make it interesting and to give him grief when he shaved. A thick crop of sandy brown hair was parted neatly on the side and clipped close above his ears and off his neck. He stood more than six feet tall and there didn't look to be an ounce of spare fat on his muscular body. The eyes were misplaced in all that masculinity, but they were as bright as the silver star pinned to his shirt pocket, and the look in them said there was a thunder storm brewing in his mood.

"Lady, I don't know who you are, but decent women in Frenchman's Ford don't play pianos in saloons. So I want you to get up and go home right now," he said. *Lord, but she was a beauty.* And when those blue eyes snapped, he swore he could see lightning streak across them in brilliant, jagged lines.

"And you are?" She pushed herself away from the piano, and stepped so close she could feel the heat of his breath on her face. Something tightened up in the pit of her stomach, something she attributed to pure anger. *How dare even the almighty sheriff come in there and make demands he had no right to.*

"I'm Sheriff Gabe Walker and I'm trying to run a clean town. So you go home," he said.

"Well, I'm Garnet Dulan and I'm not dirtying up your clean town. So you drop dead," she said.

"Don't push me, woman. What's a decent woman like you doing here, anyway?" he asked, his feathers ruffled at any woman who'd stare him right in the eye and not back down.

"Decent. Is that the problem? Well, we can fix that. You sit right down here Mr. Sheriff Gabe Walker and guard my whiskey with your badness and that star on your chest. Hey,

Jonah, help me haul my trunk in from the porch. The sheriff here doubts me and my decency," she said.

Two men were out the door and back before the Sheriff could blink. Jonah nodded up the stairs and Garnet followed them. From the look old Gabe's face when that woman bowed to him, Jonah would let her have a room just for one night. It was worth it to see his good friend Gabe out of sorts. The man made of pure steel could be taken down a peg after all and all it took was a red haired, piece of sassy baggage with a southern accent. Tomorrow she could go on down to the Widow Nash's boarding house and pay for her room, but right then a chuckle bubbled out from the depths of Jonah's chest.

"Second door on the left," Jonah said with a grin. Sheriff Gabe Walker had been his best friend for years, all the way from back when he was just plain old Gabe Walker, back when the two of them were running all over Kentucky in their bare feet and overalls. The man was doing his job, trying to clean up Frenchman's Ford. Time might come when it would be a good town, one without a homicide a day. But Gabe had met his match when he tested the mettle of Garnet Dulan. Jonah'd be willing to bet the whole Silver Dollar Saloon on that because that feisty redhead hadn't even blinked an eye when she bowed up to Gabe. Jonah swallowed an outright, full-fledged roar and wiped down the bar again. *Yep, the fireworks were about to start and the match that would light the first fuse had eyes the color of a robin's egg.*

She'd packed her yellow silk dress and all the finery that went with it on the top of the trunk so it didn't take her long to change from the blue dress she wore into the costume she'd worn in Arkansas when she played the saloon there. She slipped her black stockings up above her knees, rolled up the garters with yellow roses on them, let the yellow dress fall over her head and buttoned all the black buttons up the front, fluffing up the black lace ruffles around the low neckline and the edges of the long billowing sleeves. She slipped her feet into the high-heeled slippers she'd had custom-made. The hem of the dress, also edged in black lace teased the tops of her shoes, gave whomever wanted a peek just the slightest look at her slim ankles. Then she pulled all the pins from her red hair, letting it fall in a cascade of curls down her back to her waistline. The finishing touch was a wide lace headband tied around her forehead. It sported a plume of yellow and black feathers on the left side with several long ribbons hanging down over her ear, floating to her shoulders. She pinched her cheeks until they were nice and pink.

When she appeared at the top of the stairs, a hush filled the saloon. By the time she'd reached the bottom, the applause was so strong it rattled the glasses behind the bar and could be heard all the way across the street to the Spur Saloon. She swung the sweeping skirt tails back to one side, taking her place back on the piano bench. Sheriff Gabe Walker still stood against the side just like she'd left him, thunder still raging around in his soul and trying to escape out of eyes as clear as a blue summer sky.

"Now am I indecent enough to work this place?" she asked in a voice so icy that the sheriff almost shivered.

"Why would you want to do this?" he asked.

"Because I like it," she said and again hit the keys with force enough to resound in everyone's chest. She played "The Yellow Rose of Texas" again and several men raised their glasses in salute to her. She was truly their yellow rose, no matter where she came from. Jonah raised his own glass of sweet tea toward her. He'd hire her after all. *Yes, sir, she was going to be his ace just when he needed it.* The Spur would have a hard time keeping up with him now. Gabe could just learn to like it, because even if he argued Jonah still owned seventy-five percent of the Silver Dollar.

The sheriff shook his head and went to the bar. "Where'd you find her?" he asked Jonah. "You're askin' for trouble if you keep her, you know. She might be dolled up in that floozy dress but she's no decent woman."

"I didn't. She found me. Come strolling in here like she was born in a place like this. Made me a deal for the night. Said she'd play all night for a double shot of whiskey which she has no intentions of drinking. After that we'd negotiate a deal. I didn't think I'd hire her but I'm tempted to give her whatever she wants. I never heard nobody play like that. And she's a beauty to boot. I can already see dollar signs in the making. What do you think? Part of this place belongs to you," Jonah said.

"You might want to know something about her first," Gabe said. "She could be anyone from anywhere. She could be bringing in a load of trouble like you ain't never seen, my friend. But if you don't mind danger on the wind, then by all means hire the girl. Maybe she can even give those other four you got hired some ideas about how to look a little better."

"I wouldn't care if the devil sent her if I decide to hire her, and I was thinkin' the same thing about the other women. We might clean this joint up and make it right spiffy," Jonah told Gabe.

When the last bone-weary cowboy went home, Garnet leaned across the bar and she and Jonah began to draw up a deal. She was there on a one-week probationary period. Surely, he told himself if she really was danger, he'd know in a week. He'd give her room and board and a salary just like he did the barmaids. What she did on her own time was her business but no men were allowed past the bottom step. She'd cook every fifth day and help clean up the bar when the night was done. She was responsible for all her own laundry and whenever she wanted a bath, the tub hung on a nail on the back porch. There was a latch on the inside of the kitchen door to provide whoever was bathing with privacy, but most of the time bathing was done either after hours or before ten of a morning. That way it didn't get in the way of the cook's business for the day.

She nodded in agreement. Jonah was as fair as the last saloon owner had been and she had no complaints with the deal. She'd get to know the other girls before she started putting her other plans into action. In six months she'd have the saloon shaped up into a regular high class joint just like she'd done for the one in Arkansas, but she couldn't do it without the cooperation of Jonah and the other girls. To have that kind of cooperation, she'd have to get to know them first and they'd have to trust her.

"Deal," she said and extended her hand, and they shook on it. "I'm going up to my room and changing clothes before I help with the clean-up," she said. "Then I'm soaking in a tub until daylight."

"You go on," one of the girls said close behind her. "We'll take care of the cleaning tonight. You can start that tomorrow evening. Get you a bath. It's our way of saying thanks for playing tonight. Evening sure enough went fast with you playing that piano. I'm Rose. This is Pansy. That over there is Emmy and the short one with the blond hair is Goldie."

"Right pleased to meet you ladies," Garnet said. "And I appreciate the help tonight. I'll get my things ready and take a bath. Ain't had a tub to sit in in five months."

"Five months!" Goldie's light eyebrows arched up in disbelief.

"I've had a bath during that time," Garnet said, a smile breaking out across her pretty face. "I've been on a wagon train since the first of April, but I couldn't go on another day. So here I am and I hope we can all be friends."

"Bet we can," Rose grinned. "You better get on in the kitchen and get that bath ready. I plan on cooking us up a big skillet of eggs with onions and bacon soon as we get this job done. We usually have breakfast after we clean it up every night. Sleep until noon, eat lunch and then a light supper before the job starts. We can eat and then we'll get out of your way. Less of course, anyone wants you to leave the water for them to use."

"I doubt they'll want it tonight because I intend to use every drop of the warmth out of it," Garnet said, heading through the doors behind the bar into the kitchen area.

A long plank table took center stage with a big black cookstove in one corner and a work table in the other. Shelves held supplies as well as dishes. She'd been in fancy kitchens in big houses in Arkansas with less organization and much less cleanliness. The stove had a reservoir on the side and it was filled with good, hot water. She found the oval tub on the porch and drug it up next to the stove. Several buckets of cold water from the pump attached to the end of the dry sink, and she was ready to add hot water, but she'd wait until they ate breakfast before she did that. Like she'd said, she wasn't giving up a bit of her warmth, not even for real eggs scrambled up with onions and bacon.

Rose had begun to fry bacon when Garnet went upstairs to get her bathing sheet and soap, as well as her nightrail and shawl. The smell of frying onions wafted up the stairs and her stomach growled as she opened the door into her room. Home. That's what she felt when she stood in the middle of the room. So much like the one in Arkansas. A big feather bed over there under the window where the night breezes blew in through the plain white curtain. A dresser with a small mirror. A real luxury after living out in the open for the past several months. Clean sheets and blankets folded at the end of the bed. She'd make it later after she'd eaten and had her bath.

Yes, sir, Garnet Dulan had made the right decision when she left the wagon train. A tear hung on her long lashes for just a moment when she remembered the good-byes she'd had to endure with her sister, Gussie, who'd have to finish the trip alone. She wiped it away. She'd miss Gussie, all right. But even the love she had for her sister couldn't make her complete that trip and marry some man she'd never met before. She simply could not promise to love, honor and obey some gold miner who'd paid money for her. If she ever gave her vows in marriage, it would be to someone who paid for her with his heart, not his money.

Last spring, she and her four sisters had been called from five different states—Pennsylvania, Texas, North Carolina, Arkansas and Tennessee to Saint Joseph, Missouri to their father, Jake Dulan's deathbed—only to arrive too late and just in time for the funeral. In his will, he told them they were sisters. None of them had known they had siblings until that time, but the strange aqua blue eyes they shared left no doubt that although they'd had different mothers, they'd sure enough shared the same father who'd had the same color eyes. Jake Dulan had been in partnership with Hank Gibson, running wagon trains from St. Jo to California. Hank had taken on the job of taking more than a hundred women from Missouri to a little town the miners called Bryte. The miners had paid good money to have the mail order brides brought to them. The Dulan sisters signed on with the agreement with Hank that when they arrived in California if there were more than a hundred women, they'd step down and not demand a husband out of the deal. Garnet never intended to go the full distance; never intended to marry a man she'd never met, one she didn't love.

The youngest sister, Willow, fell in love with Rafe Pierce, one of the hired hands and left to live in Nebraska with him after they were married. Velvet, the middle sister, took a fever and one of the trailhands left her in Fort Laramie, where she married the doctor who'd cared for her. Gypsy Rose had left the train just a few weeks before to go to Chalk Creek, Utah Territory to marry a little short Irishman and help him with his horse ranch. That just left Gussie and Garnet. When the train reached the outskirts of Frenchman's Ford, Garnet made her decision to stay right there.

Things were working out even better and faster than she'd imagined. She had a job, a room that she could call her own even if it was for a week only, and the makings of a warm bath in the kitchen. She could sleep until noon the next day. She'd put that blue-eyed sheriff in his place and nothing could possibly go wrong. Yes, sir, she was going to love Frenchman's Ford. And at the end of the week, Jonah would hire her on indefinitely.

She picked up her bundle of clothing, and with a step lighter than she'd known in several months, almost floated down the stairs to get to know the other girls. Rose, Emmy, Goldie and Pansy. She could already envision the colors of the satin dresses she intended to sew for them. The brightest hot pink for Rose. She'd look like a real rose in bright pink with all that gorgeous black hair and dark eyes. A rich emerald green for Emmy to enhance her green eyes. Yellow for Goldie with the blond hair and brown eyes. And deep purple for Pansy. Colors to go with their names and the patrons of the Silver Dollar would know them by the colors before a week was finished. Garnet would fashion herself a deep red dress to go along with her name. It would take a couple of weeks, but she could already foresee the sight of the five of them making their grand entrance.

By the time they got to that stage of her plans, Jonah would be so excited with the till every evening, he'd be willing to let Garnet handle the girls and the piano. She smiled as she opened the kitchen door. *No sir, not one thing could go wrong now.* Even the girls' names and looks had fallen into her plans. It couldn't have been better if she'd owned the Silver Dollar herself.

Chapter Two

T he sun was high and warm rays found their way around the curtain edges to spin gracious patterns on the top of the homemade quilt. Garnet awoke to the smell of coffee drifting up the steps and under her closed door. She stretched like a lazy cat, wiggling down into the clean sheets and shutting her eyes, enjoying the feel of a feather bed. Reaching out to catch the warmth of the sun on her fingertips, she threw back the covers and pushed the curtains aside, looking down onto the busy main street of town. Frenchman's Ford looked just like any other small town in the daylight. A general store across the street from the Silver Dollar. A church up on the corner. A bank just up the street from the Silver Dollar with a white house with pink trim beside it. *Could that be the Jezebel's that Jasper mentioned last night? Well, if it was, Jezebel kept her place in good repair.* The good sheriff went inside the jailhouse and then reappeared a few minutes later, a determination in his step as he crossed the street diagonally. Looked as if he was on his way to the Silver Dollar with something on his mind.

Garnet smiled. The almighty Sheriff Gabe Walker wouldn't have any better luck running her out of town in the broad daylight than he'd had while the stars twinkled overhead. She chose the first dress on the top of the trunk to wear that morning. A faded calico that had been bright blue sprinkled with tiny red roses. Days and days of walking twelve to fifteen miles a day in the hot blistering sun had faded it to a washed out light blue with scarcely any sign of a rosebud left. By the time she reached the kitchen, Sheriff Gabe Walker was there. Pure old unadulterated thunder danced out of his eyes when she walked through the door in her bare feet.

"Miss Garnet Dulan, you are under the arrest for the robbery of the Ullin bank and for the murder of the teller in that bank two days ago. Are you going to come with me peacefully or am I going to have to . . ."

All the color drained from her face and she had to grab the back of Rose's chair to keep from falling flat on her face in the middle of the kitchen floor. This was a joke to repay her for her brazenness the night before. She took a deep breath and forced the room to stop spinning. "That's not funny," she said in a hoarse whisper.

"No it's not," the sheriff said. "A man is dead and there's hundreds of dollars missing from the bank. I'll be going through your things up there as soon as I have you behind bars. Now come along with me."

"I'm barefoot," she said, and wondered suddenly if she could escape out the window and across the roof of the building when he let her go back to her room for her shoes.

"You won't need shoes in my jail," Gabe said seriously, grabbing her by the arm.

"I was on a wagon train headed for California two days ago. I've been on it since April. Hank Gibson can tell you that. He'll only be a few miles down the road this morning. Go ask him," she jerked her arm free of Gabe's fingers.

"I don't have to go looking for your alibi, lady. I just have to lock you up until the only witness at the bank robbery gets here to identify you. He'll know if you're the red-haired woman who pulled the trigger on that shotgun and killed that man." Gabe took her arm again, this time gripping hard enough that she couldn't jerk free. He'd

known when he saw her things weren't right. Something
had tightened up in his gut so strong he'd almost quit
breathing.

"Probation is over," Jonah said. "Even if that man says
you are innocent, I won't hire you. Can't have every gun-
slinger in town coming in to take a look at the woman who
was arrested. No hard feelings, Garnet. You play a mean
piano and I hope that witness backs up your story, but you
ain't workin' here. I can't have my saloon shot up every
night because men folks are fighting over whether the piano
player is innocent or guilty."

Garnet tugged against the fingers digging into the soft
flesh on her upper arm, but Gabe's hold didn't weaken. He
led her across the dusty street and up three steps to the
wooden sidewalk. She got a splinter in the bottom of her
tender foot, but she didn't say a word because down deep
in her heart she knew it wouldn't do a bit of good. Not
with this sorry excuse for a man. He hadn't wanted her at
the saloon the night before and she'd made him a laughing
stock. Now she had no job and was accused of robbery and
murder. That brought a hanging in Nevada Territory, she
was sure. Her stomach rolled but she fought back the gag-
ging reflex of pure fear when he opened the jailhouse door.
The room he drug her into was smaller than the one she'd
slept in the night before. A wooden desk covered with pa-
pers of all kinds took center stage. A couple of mismatched
chairs were positioned in front of it with a bigger one behind it. On each side of that room were two barred rooms—
jail cells.

Garnet had never been behind bars in her life. She'd been
inside the sheriff's office more than once, testifying that
Old Tom Tuttle had gotten too much whiskey in his gullet
and shot up the place, or that young Ivy Tuttle had gotten
too much whiskey in his gullet and tried to cheat at cards.
Usually the sheriff gave them a cell for the night and David
Tuttle, the son of Tom and father of Ivy would ride into
town the next day and pay their fines.

"We'll give you this end." Gabe picked up a ring of keys. "We'll keep the men folks over there unless it gets crowded next Saturday night. You might have to share your cell with a few drunks then."

Garnet glared at him, her eyes flashing more lightning than his could re-echo with thunder. "I did not rob a bank or kill anyone. A two-hour ride down the wagon trail could prove both. I was on that train until last night. Bobby, the Indian scout, brought me into town and put my trunk on the porch of the Silver Dollar."

"Sure, honey. And I bet Bobby, the Indian scout, would tell everyone that. But who's going to listen to an Indian?" Gabe shoved her into a tiny cell with a straw mattress on a wooden cot, a slop jar in the corner and a bucket of water beside it. A tiny window with five bars let in a bit of the afternoon sun, trying desperately to spread a little bit of warmth in the cold stone walls of the cell.

She brushed the mouse droppings from the mattress with the back of her hand and sat down, pulling her skirt tails around her ankles tightly so if the mouse did come back for a visit it wouldn't run up under her dress. The stones were rough and chilly against her backbone but she could either lean on them or fall out in the middle of the floor in a dead faint.

She wouldn't give Gabe Walker that satisfaction.

He disappeared after a few minutes at his desk. Most likely to go through her things. He'd find less than a hundred dollars in her chest, and only that if he looked hard enough to find the false bottom. A few faded dresses. Her fancy yellow dress was still draped over the top where she'd left it last night. Why oh why hadn't she taken those letters from Gussie when she'd offered them the day before? They would have proven she'd been on the train. But the good Sheriff Walker wouldn't find them. Just a lady's normal packing. Unmentionables, brush and comb set, a small mirror . . . and her sweet little pistol she carried every where she went.

She moaned when she remembered the gun.

"Well, you the one who killed the bank teller over in Ullin?" a short, portly fellow asked he threw his hat on the desk.

"I didn't kill anyone," Garnet said, her voice an octave higher than normal.

"Sure you didn't, honey. Sure you didn't. Everyone behind them bars is innocent. Never had a one of them that was guilty. Course that didn't keep us from hanging a good many of them. And women don't have no special rights in Nevada Territory. You kill someone and you die for it," the man said. "I'm Deputy Les Watkins. We got us a witness coming over from Ullin. Be here in a couple of days and he'll sure enough tell us you're the redhead who did the dirty deed. That teller had a young wife and a baby not a year old. How's that make you feel?"

Garnet shut her eyes and ignored the man. Just how much did that witness see? Was it dark? Could he tell the sheriff that Garnet was definitely not the woman who'd fired that gun? Or would he look at her, decide all redheads looked the same and give the nod of death?

"You even want to know the name of the teller?" The Deputy stood close to the bars and glared at her. "You 'bout one cold-hearted hussy. Witness said the teller just looked up and said, 'Why?' and you blew a hole in his chest a body could drive a freight wagon through."

Garnet shook her head. She didn't want to know his name or even why someone killed him. She just wanted out of this cell. She'd even join back with the wagon train and marry a man she didn't know if she could end this horrible nightmare.

"You are cold blooded," the deputy snarled then returned to the desk. "Women is supposed to be gentle and homemakers, not killers and saloon girls."

Sure they were, Garnet drew her knees up close enough she could rest her chin on them. If the world was as perfect as men thought they'd made it, all women could be gentle and homemakers. They wouldn't die, leaving behind children to be raised by relatives who didn't want them. They'd be pampered and loved with tenderness and kindness. But as bad as she hated to burst the deputy's little flawless bubble, women had to be hard as nails sometimes. They had to carve their own way out of an unforgiving, hard, cold world, and they had to do it in spite of men, not with their help.

The scraping sound of wood against wood reached her ears before the door opened and Sheriff Walker drug her rolltop chest into the middle of the jail house. He'd clamped the top down on her feather headpiece, part of it fluttering with the breeze he'd created by slamming the door shut. "Well, honey, you must've buried the money somewhere else, because there ain't a single dime in that trunk. But I did find this. You got some hair-brained explanation for why you're carrying around a gun? I mean other than to use to rob a bank and kill a young man?" Gabe held the gun up to the bars.

"It's my gun. I've had it for years. Bought it in Arkansas when I worked at the saloon there. It's not safe for a woman to be out on the streets at night without protection," she said.

"A likely story," Gabe chuckled. "And probably the truth. You also used it to kill a man. You should've buried it along with your part of the money. Now we got a murder weapon. Soon as the witness gets here, he'll tell us this was the gun, too."

"I'm so sure that little popgun could blow a hole in a man big enough to drive a freight wagon through," Garnet said, never taking her eyes from his. She'd sing a hymn while they hanged her from the gallows before she let that egotistical man intimidate her.

"So you admit you killed him, then?" Gabe raised an eyebrow.

"I don't admit to anything. I wasn't even near whatever town you are talking about. I was on a wagon train until late last evening, and if you weren't so full of yourself, you'd send that fat deputy over there out to the wagon train before it gets too far away and check my story. My sister is still on it. Gussie Dulan is her name. Hank is the wagon master. He's taking a hundred women to California to marry the gold miners there," she said.

"Yes, he is," Gabe said. "I know all about that train. Everybody knows about that train, but you wasn't on it. You was in Ullin in amongst a murderous gang of three, robbing the bank and killing a man. Who were the two men with you? Give us their names and we might go easy on you. Might just lock you up until all that pretty red hair turns white instead of stretching out that lovely neck with a rope."

"Hang her. She got no business calling me fat," the deputy said, pulling himself up in an effort to make his round stomach disappear.

"I couldn't tell you the two men's names because I wasn't there," Garnet said.

"Your call," the sheriff said. "I'll just put this away for evidence. The judge will be here day after tomorrow. You're a lucky woman. He's a circuit judge. Only makes it through Frenchman's Ford every other month. You could've been enjoying the view from behind those bars for two months if we'd a caught you in three more days. Witness should be here tomorrow night pretty late. He'll be in the court with the judge the next morning. Reckon we can probably get the hanging over with by noon that day."

Garnet ignored him but she couldn't ignore the icy fingers of dread producing shivers up her back bone.

The minutes passed slowly. The hours lasted an eternity. By noon she'd dug the splinter out of the sole of her foot with her fingernails, and had begun to pace the floor for exercise. What she'd give to be walking along beside their wagon couldn't be measured in anything tangible. To read the three letters from their sisters, telling all about their lives and how much they were in love. To listen to little Merry Wilson asking a thousand questions in a day. To worry if there would be water that night for bathing and laundry. Anything. Anywhere but in a jail cell waiting to be hung for a crime she didn't commit.

The sun was setting when a woman walked through the door carrying a basket. She wore a pristine navy blue dress with only the faintest touch of hand-crocheted lace at the collar. Mousy brown hair was pulled back severely from her plain face into a bun at the nape of her neck. A slat bonnet hung down her back, the ties in a neat bow right under her chin.

"I'm Betsy, the preacher's wife," she said with a sweet smile. "I cook for the prisoners when there are any. I've brought you some supper. A bowl of potato soup and a half a loaf of bread."

"I'll unlock it, but you be careful. She's a cold killer, that one is," the deputy said.

"Just let me in and lock it back up. I'll stay with her while she eats," Betsy said.

"It's your fault if she tries to kill you," he said.

"What with? A spoon?" Betsy laughed.

The sound of that feminine giggle did more to raise Garnet's spirits than if the woman had come in brandishing a shot gun and demanding that the prisoner be let go free. Betsy spread the napkin from the top of the basket on Garnet's lap, opened up the jar of soup and poured it into a bowl, handed her a spoon and sat down on the end of the bed.

"I did not kill anyone and I didn't rob that bank," Garnet said before she ever took the first bite.

"I'm not here to judge you, Miss Dulan. I'm here to bring you food. Eat now and we'll talk," Betsy said. "Why are you barefoot?"

Garnet put the first bite of the warm soup in her mouth and shut her eyes in appreciation. It seemed like a month had passed since she'd eaten the scrambled eggs the night before. "Because the good sheriff didn't trust me to go upstairs and put my shoes on. They're in that trunk over there but no one has offered to get them for me."

"Unlock this door right now," Betsy said.

"Be glad to. I told you she was a killer. You figured it out for yourself, did you?" the deputy said, clinking the key into the lock and letting the woman out.

She shot him a look meant to drop him in his tracks, but he didn't have enough brains to recognize it and kept up a steady stream of advice against women who didn't know their place. Betsy tried to ignore him as she opened the trunk and found Garnet's worn shoes. She pulled everything out, folded it neatly in front of the deputy, and with the shoes and a pair of stockings in her hands, went back to the cell. "Now let me back in," she demanded.

"You are crazy as she is," he said flatly.

"Maybe so, but you are not God. So stop playing like it. What happened to innocent until proven guilty?" Betsy threw back at him.

"Oh, she's guilty all right," he said.

"Ignore him. He's not fit to be a deputy. I don't know why Gabe hired him. Probably because a man with any sense wouldn't take the job. Not after Joe Nash got killed a few months ago right outside the jailhouse door. We've got at least two killings a week right here in Frenchman's Ford. It's a sorry place to raise kids and bring women, but Gabe is trying his best to clean it up. It'll be a fine town someday, and we're working hard at the church to put people on the right track. Now put them feet down here, Miss Garnet, I intend to wash them and help you get your boots on. It'll be cold tonight and you'll catch your death in this old cold stone building."

"Thank you," Garnet brushed away a tear. "I'm innocent. I just want you to know that."

"It's not my business to judge. Jesus himself didn't condemn the woman they brought to him in adultery. But I believe you," Betsy said, getting about the task of washing

Garnet's feet. "I'll bring you a warm blanket before I go to bed."

"Thank you again," Garnet said.

The half hour that Betsy was there with her went by in a flash. True to her word, Betsy came back in an hour with a thick patchwork quilt which Garnet wrapped tightly around her when she stretched out on the cot. When she looked out the window she saw that the moon was a big white ball with five distinct lines across it—five iron bars that kept Garnet inside a cold, damp, little room not even as big as the wagon she and four or five other women had lived in for the past months. The difference was that she could get out of the wagon and see the moon in all its glory.

It was close to sunrise before she slept and then it was to dream of a man with blue eyes putting a rope around her neck and laughing while he did it. She awoke in a cold sweat to find mouse droppings on the mattress all around her. So the critter had come back to visit and she'd not even known it was there. Thank goodness the sham would be over in two days. Even if the witness said she was the one in the bank and they hanged her, it would be over. She couldn't take two months of life in a cell, or a life sentence. Death didn't look nearly so bad when she considered the alternative.

Betsy arrived sometime after daybreak with breakfast, stayed a half an hour and left. She told her about Frenchman's Ford. They had a school there but the last teacher had left a month before. The town only had a handful of womenfolk, and none of them were able to teach the fifteen kids who needed an education. Four of the women worked at the Silver Dollar Saloon and four more at the Spur. Jezebel brought her own women when she set up the bawdy house, Betsy said in whispers.

Betsy said that she could teach, but if she did, she'd be taking away from the ministry she and her husband were attempting to set up in Frenchman's Ford. So most of the children were taught what little lessons they got at home.

Garnet watched the pendulum swing back and forth, back and forth on the big clock in the corner as she waited for lunch. The food wasn't as important as Betsy's visit— that time she told her about how she and her husband, Matthew, had come from West Virginia to Nevada; The Lord had called them to go to the frontier and bring souls to God; they had a daughter, Charity, who was nine years old with red hair, pretty close to the color of Garnet's, and a constant propensity for getting into trouble and two sons, Daniel and Joshua, who were five and six, and, praise the Lord, didn't have their sister's temper or red hair.

The clock's pendulum swung slow all afternoon. Gabe was in and out but he mostly just glared at her. He tripped over the trunk once and kicked it soundly, uttered a few words under his breath, and again, she thought of thunder when he scowled at her. She remembered something one of her aunts said many years before. Garnet was just a child, and she'd run to the aunt's bedside, fearful of the horrible storm threatening to rip up half of Arkansas.

"Don't be afraid of the thunder, Garnet," the aunt said. "It's just noise. It's lightning you must fear. It's silent and deadly. Can strike anywhere, anytime. Thunder is just the echo of the power that lightning has."

So he flashed thunder in those blue eyes, did he? Well, that wasn't anything but empty noise.

She ate a healthy supper and wrapped herself in the quilt again, said a brief prayer that the mouse wouldn't come around or would be so quiet she didn't hear it. That's all the night deputy needed: a story to tell everyone about the icy killer in his jail cell who could shoot a man down in cold blood but was afraid of a little mouse.

The witness would be in town by now. Probably sleeping in the boarding house Betsy mentioned down the street from the jail. Tomorrow the judge would arrive. Three days ago she was on a wagon train bound for California. Nothing made a bit of sense. She looked at the striped moon and shut her eyes, expecting to lay there for hours before the nightmares began again.

Sleep came instantly.

Westville Public Library
Westville, IL 61883

Chapter Three

Garnet thought she was dreaming when the noise awoke her. In her dream, the night deputy had fallen out of his chair when he went to sleep. She opened her eyes slowly, hoping there wasn't a mouse sleeping on the mattress with her like she'd seen in the dream. Before she could get things in focus, the door of the jail cell swung wide open and a big, burly man had his hand tangled up in her hair.

"Wake up lady and say your prayers because tonight you are going to hang," he said gruffly, pulling her to her feet. "Not a sound. Not even a peep or I'll let Josie over there take care of the whole thing right here in this jail cell."

Garnet figured it was another nightmare, but the pain from her hair being yanked by the roots told her quickly this was no dream, even if it was as scary as any nightmare she'd ever had.

"Who are you?" she managed to say as the man marched her out of the cell and to the door.

He flung the door open and looked both ways before he shoved her outside. "Crawl up on that horse, and don't you make a sound, woman, or I'll blow your face off right here. Don't make no difference if we string up a dead body or a live one."

Garnet slung one leg over the saddled horse. There were

24

three of them—a woman in a hat that covered most of her features, but it was evident she was a very small lady, the big, burly man who'd cold-cocked the deputy and kid-napped her from the cell, and a tall, thin man who with a full black beard and long, shaggy dark hair. *Who were they?* Why were they so intend on breaking her out of jail? And were they really going to hang her?

She swallowed hard and grabbed at the reins but the big man got to them first. "Don't you even try it, woman. Don't make me no difference how you die. Josie just thinks you oughta hang so it'll look like a vigilante bunch."

"Who are you?" Garnet asked again, but there were no answers as the man led her horse out at a gentle walk to-ward the west. Once outside of town, he drew the whole bunch of them up under a tree. In spite of the cool night breeze, sweat ran down Garnet's back in a steady stream. She inhaled deeply, the smell of the night filling her lungs, then she exhaled, and forgot to breath again until her chest began to ache. There would be no trial, no witnesses, noth-ing. Just a rope and the end. She watched the man make a noose from a length of new rope he had fixed to his saddle horn. She could either sit still or stiffen up her Dulan spine and take matters in her own hands.

"Why are you doing this?" She asked.

"Because we need a dead redhead for that witness to identify tomorrow," the woman said. "After we hang you, I'm going to blow your face away with this shotgun. Then it will be finished."

Two guns were trained on her—one a double barreled shotgun, the other a powerful looking pistol even in the light of the full moon. A noose was being made and she had a choice. Let them hang her or take a one in a thousand chance that she could dodge a bunch of lead. She chose the latter; grabbed the reins, kneed the horse and took off in a dead run, expecting to hear the pop of the tall man's gun and the blast from the woman's. When neither happened, she chanced a look over her left shoulder just in time to see a big, beefy hand reach and grab her hair. The horse kept running and she was slammed to the ground, the tall man on top of her so fast she wondered what had happened.

"Don't you try that again, woman," he said in a voice that bore absolutely no warmth. "We ain't playin' games here. You are a dead woman and there's not a thing you can do about it. We're just glad old stupid Gabe found you. Makes our little robbery and murder a done deal."

"You mean, you robbed that bank?" she huffed, beginning to understand why they needed her. Up under that woman's wide-brimmed cowboy hat must be a full head of red hair.

"Sure did, honey. And we're going to get away with it, too," he said, standing up and kicking her soundly in the ribs.

She sucked air but kept the tears at bay. She'd just proven she couldn't outrun them but maybe she could outsmart them. At least she thought she could, until he filled his hands with her hair again and pulled her up beside him, only to clamp a set of hand cuffs on her wrists.

Arms cuffed behind her back, ribs aching, he marched her back to the tree where the noose dangled right in front of her. The big man pulled on it until it was the right height and motioned for the woman to get off her horse.

"Use your own horse. You're already off it," Josie said in a surly voice. "I'll take care of the shooting when she's dangling. You two wouldn't have the stomach for that."

"You're a cold-blooded one," the man chuckled. "Get her on my horse. I'm not afraid to ride an animal that's took care of a killing like sweet little Josie is. Besides, she ain't going to be needin' the horse but a minute. Just long enough to take care of this business."

The skinny man picked her up, ignored all the kicking and screaming, and set her soundly in the saddle of the big chestnut-colored horse. She tried wiggling her head but the big man slapped her firmly across the face and while she was dazed, he slipped the rope around her neck. Josie threw her hat off her head, letting it drop by the strings down her back, not unlike the way Garnet had worn her bonnet on the days when she walked beside the wagon on the trail with the rest of the Dulan women. Josie held the shotgun tightly against her shoulder and took aim at where Garnet's head would be when the horse left her hanging.

There's only four sisters now, Garnet thought as the horse fidgeted, eager to get rid of the unknown woman on his back. *Will they come and visit my grave? Will someone let them know I've died and will they believe I was innocent? Good-bye, my dear sisters.*

"Let's get it done," the woman said. "Hit the horse. I've got her in my sights."

"Who are you?" Garnet asked. "Surely you can tell me that. I'm going to die. At least give me the satisfaction of knowing whose place I'm taking."

"Why, I'm the grieving widow of that spineless coward in the bank. I knew there was a big shipment of money coming in, and I knew better than to ask him to help me rob the bank. Him and his pious ways. He would have shot himself before he would do something illegal. He didn't have to die, but he recognized me right there at the end. Just as well. I'd planned on leaving him anyway. Now he don't have to be heartsick as well as a coward," she laughed.

"There's a witness. He'll know I'm not the one he saw," Garnet said, the rope beginning to choke her even as she sat there, her arms behind her, afraid to breathe for fear the horse would jump. If only she could keep them talking, maybe the deputy would awaken and go for help or better yet, jump on his horse, bring his gun and take care of matters himself.

Sure he will, her conscience said. *He thinks you are guilty. He'll probably wait until tomorrow to even tell Gabe you were broke out and then he'll say that they were just taking you because you're one of them.*

"The witness is a scared kid. Twelve years old. He'll

look at a woman with her face blown away with a shot gun and see red hair and say it was you in that bank. Right after he pukes in the rosebushes, that is," Josie laughed wickedly. "Hit that horse, Luke, and then go round it up so we can ride out of here."

"What about your baby?" Garnet asked.

"My baby?" Josie laughed again, this time more shrill and hysterical. "My baby will be fine with my parents. I left them a note telling them that I couldn't bear to live there any longer with the memories. To take good care of the child. I never wanted to be a mother anyway."

Hot tears flowed down Garnet's cheeks. Another baby for relatives to raise who'd grow up without a father or a mother. She hoped it wasn't a girlchild. She heard the slap on rump of the big animal and suddenly she was hanging. Her neck hadn't snapped but she couldn't breathe. The rope cut into her neck and tightened with every swing. She tried to be very still and not panic but it was futile. The moon, this time without the stripes of the bars of the cell window, faded around the edges and she heard Josie thumb back both hammers of the shotgun. A loud blast filled the air around her and everything went black.

Les rubbed his head and brought back a bloody hand. He was on the sidewalk by the time the jail breakers reached the end of the street and running toward the widow's boarding house before they broke into a trot. He stormed in without knocking, stumbled up the stairs, yelling like a wounded buffalo for Gabe, who met him in the hallway.

"Someone just broke that Dulan woman out of jail. They said they were going to take her outside of town and hang her. I heard that much before I passed out completely," he held his head and talked loudly.

"Which way did they go? West? There's only one tree out that way big enough for a hanging. You get us a couple of horses saddled up and make it in a hurry, Les. I'll wake up that kid who's a witness and we'll get on out there," Gabe said. "I knew that woman was trouble the first time I met her. Well, what are you waiting for? A gold gilded invitation to a hanging? Get going, man."

Les got going, still holding his pounding head and mumbling to himself. It was probably a wild goose chase. They'd most likely circled back around and headed back to the east or the south and while the deputy and the sheriff were standing under a lonesome old tree, they'd be laughing their heads off at them. But he'd do what the sheriff said because that was his job.

Gabe hoisted the young boy up on the horse in front of him. The kid was literally shaking in his boots. Gabe hadn't had much time to talk to him but the boy was fearful that his father was going to flay the hide off his back for going to town on a day when he was supposed to be plowing.

They rode fast and furious toward the tree—a mile outside of town where Gabe figured the vigilantes had taken Garnet Dulan. He wasn't surprised. Not really. A woman didn't kill a good, gentle man and get away with it. It would save him and Frenchman's Ford the cost of a trial and get the whole thing over with. He didn't care if she was dead, but that wasn't the way the law read, so he'd ride out there and try to prevent the hanging.

They heard a lot of screaming and the blast from a shotgun, then three horses rode past them; fast, in a big hurry and the boy yelled back to Gabe that the killer was getting away. Gabe pulled up the reins and stopped the horse.

"It's the woman in the bank. The red haired woman I saw. Her bandanna fell down like I told you just for a minute when she jumped on her horse and her hat flew backwards. It's that woman riding away right there," he pointed to the south where the riders were getting away.

Gabe looked at the human body swinging from the tree, red hair flowing in the gentle night winds. So they'd killed Garnet Dulan, and he'd been wrong.

"Cut her down, Les," he said. "And take care of this kid. I'm going after them."

Les nodded. Lord, he hated to touch dead people. He rode up close, being careful not to let his hands near the body and with one swift slice, he cut the rope right above her ear. She tumbled to the ground with a thud. Gabe could just wait until morning and send the undertaker out there in his wagon to gather up the body. Wasn't no way Les was going to walk all the way back to town because he had a dead woman draped over his saddle. He was sure that it would bring bad luck for a dead person to touch his saddle. Not that he'd ever heard such a thing, but there had to be something about it somewhere, and Les wasn't taking any chances when it came to bad luck.

"Come on boy," he held his hand down to boy who leaped up behind him. "We'll get you back to town and into bed. That deputy who brought you down here can take you back tomorrow. Don't look like there's going to be no trial."

"They done killed the wrong woman," the kid said. "That woman is taller than the one who killed that man. She's got longer hair," his voice broke and he sobbed, "They done killed the wrong one."

"Well, it's too late now to be cryin' over a dead woman. You didn't even know her boy," Les said.

"That woman looked like my momma did when she was dead. My momma was that size. A tall woman. My daddy loved her so much, and now she's dead. That wasn't the one who killed that man. Why'd you put her in jail anyway? It's your fault," the boy said between sobs.

"It ain't our fault, kid," Les said but his voice didn't sound convincing. "We was just doing our duty. The woman shows up the same time we hear there's been a killing. She fits the description we got so we arrested her and waited for you to come identify her."

"Why didn't you protect her better?" he asked. "You didn't do your job."

Les couldn't answer him.

Gabe rode hard, but in a matter of a few minutes, it was evident he was losing ground. They disappeared out of his sight and tracking them in the night, even with the light of the moon, would be a futile effort. *Garnet was dead.* They knew the woman with red hair and two companions were still on the loose. He'd send Les and a posse out at daybreak to see if they could pick up the trail.

With a heavy heart he rode back to the hanging tree, expecting to find Les waiting for him. He'd been wrong a few times in his life, but never had it cost the life of an innocent woman. All it would've taken was a few hours to send Les down to that wagon train to ask a few questions, but oh, no, he'd been the big, important sheriff. The one who'd gotten his toes stepped on in the Silver Dollar that night when she'd given him a healthy dose of comeuppance. He examined his own conscience to see if that was the real reason he'd been so quick to judge her and came up with an answer he didn't like.

Les' horse wasn't silhouetted against the big, full moon. Gabe drew his eyes down in a squint, but he couldn't make that horse appear. Evidently, he'd draped Garnet's body over the horse and taken her back into town. He'd already pulled the reins to turn his horse back to town when he noticed the thin line dangling from the tree. It looked strange hanging there like a fine pencil line across the drawing of a big round moon. He didn't want to face Betsy tomorrow when she lambasted him for Garnet's death so he wasn't in a hurry to get back to Frenchman's Ford. He rode up to the tree slowly with plans of taking the rope down. Anything to keep from riding back into town with the weight of guilt riding heavily on his shoulders. What had Garnet thought of in her last moments? And why had they shot her? He dreaded looking at the body tomorrow. Garnet Diana Dulan had been a lovely woman, she'd made his own blood hot. Looking at her broken and shot all to pieces wasn't going to be easy.

He reached for the rope and his horse sidestepped something on the ground. Gabe looked down to see the woman lying there in a heap. "Blast that Les. I'm going to fire him first thing in the morning. If I have to do all the work and keep the jail myself twenty four hours a day, I'll do it," he grumbled loudly as he dismounted. At least he had someone to rage at other than himself.

He'd pick her up and drape her over his own saddle. A good long walk to town might atone for his sins. She was still very warm and rigor hadn't set in when he unfolded her body from the way she'd fallen when Les cut her down and left her for the wolves and coyotes to feed upon. Gabe dreaded turning her over, fully expecting to see the effects of the shotgun either on her face or her chest. But when he eased her onto her back, it was only to look down into the ashen beautiful face of the woman who'd been so sassy to him at the Silver Dollar. He quickly checked her body for blood and found none, just a streak on her temple and that didn't look like a graze but more like a skin break from a hard slap or a fall. So she'd fought them or tried to escape. Well, that sure fit in with the image he got of her that night at the Silver Dollar. A determined woman who wouldn't let anyone get the best of her. But they had, in the end. It took three of them but they'd sure enough gotten the best of Garnet.

He slipped the rope from her neck, staring for a long time at the bloody whelp it had made on her slender throat. He was reaching out to touch it, to apologize even to her after death, when she convulsed, a shudder shaking her entire body. He jumped like someone had shot at him. The last of the pent up air in her lungs. He'd seen it before in the dead. Sometimes it took a while for that one last shiver. Whoever fired off those shots must have been shooting at him and Les. Thank goodness they hadn't killed that young kid. Then he'd have the blood of two innocent people dirtying his hands.

Gabe used his cuff key to unlock the cuffs from around her wrists, rubbed at the red bruises there, and then reminded himself that they'd be there forever. Garnet was dead. He slipped an arm under her hips and one around her shoulders and lifted her to his chest. It wasn't easy mounting the horse with her in his arms, but he finally got the job done. Then he began a slow ride back to town where he fully intended to have Les' badge by dinnertime the next day.

He rode up to the undertaker's house, threw a leg over the saddle and very ungracefully got down, hoisting the dead weight of the woman who'd been so full of life and vigor just hours before. He carried her to the door and kicked it violently with his foot.

"I'm a comin'. I'm a comin'," someone said inside the house then the door swung open. "Who is it?"

"Garnet Diana Dulan," Gabe said. "The woman I had in the jail. Vigilantes hung her."

"Well, I heard she done killed a man. Lay her over there on the table. I'll take care of her at daylight. Going to put her in the pauper's part of the graveyard, I guess?" the undertaker scratched at his bald head and yawned.

"No, I want a full funeral. Betsy will bring her clothes tomorrow. The woman was innocent. That witness who came from Ullin said she wasn't the one in the bank," Gabe said, avoiding the man's eyes, and laying Garnet's body out gently on the big wooden table in the corner.

"Well, if that don't beat all," the undertaker said. "Well, she can stay there until morning and you and Betsy can come tell me what to do with her. Church and all?"

"All of it. Church. Flowers. A wreath on the hearse and a bunch of songs. She'd like that. Garnet would like songs, Floyd. Get the ladies from the church to sing," Gabe said.

"Well, all right," Floyd said.

Just the whisper of a moan made both men's hearts jump nearly out of their chests. Floyd ran across the floor to the table and laid a hand on Garnet's neck, then grabbed up her wrist. "Gabe, this woman is alive. Barely, but she's alive. Didn't you check for a heartbeat or a pulse before you brung her here to me? You better go get the doctor and hurry up about it. She ain't dead. Not yet."

Chapter Four

Sun rays feathered through the rose pattern on the curtains hanging in the window, and cast playful patterns on the snowy white coverlet pulled up around Garnet's waist. Her first thought when she opened her eyes was that she'd just had the mother of all nightmares. A horrible thing about being hung and dying. Then she tried to swallow and the pain began. Even the simple act of swallowing was a chore, not to mention the way her head pounded with every heart beat. And those things were minor compared to the stabbing pain in her ribs when she tried to take a breath.

It had not been a nightmare after all. They'd kicked her, slapped her, hung her and it was only the pure grace of God that they hadn't shot her right in the face. She knew she'd lived through it all, because there wouldn't be this much pain in death. Right now, she felt like the only surviving chicken at the finish of a wild coyote party. She gingerly touched the bandage around her neck and winced, only the faintest of moans escaping her lips.

"Well, well, I guess you done returned from the land of the dead," a deep voice said just off to her left. She turned her head slowly in that direction. She certainly wasn't back in jail. Not unless they'd hung lace curtains over the windows since she'd swung from a rope out at the edge of town. She wasn't back in her old room over the saloon, either. It hadn't been nearly so nice.

"Your eyes are open, but I 'spect you're feelin' poorly after that close walk down the valley of the shadow of death. Well, it just might be the very thing that puts you on the straight and narrow," the voice said.

Garnet finally brought her eyes into focus and stared impolitely at the woman with the deepest, most Southern voice she'd ever heard. "Where am I?" she whispered, her own voice even deeper and as raspy as the woman's.

"You are at my boarding house, Garnet Dulan. I'm Stella Nash and Sheriff Gabe brought you here in the wee hours of the morning after the doctor declared you were alive. Guess you gave him a start there for a while," Stella laughed. "But it was only good enough for him. Struttin' around like he's God, himself. Well, honey, you done knocked him right off his big fluffy white cloud. Never have seen a man so sorry in all my life. But don't you go forgivin' him too quick. Make him beg and squirm a while. Man deserves to squirm. After all he owns part of one of those vile saloons up the street."

"He is a skunk. Never forgive him," Garnet managed to eke out before her voice played completely out.

"Don't try to talk now," Stella said. "I'm going downstairs and rustle you up some chicken broth. Doctor says you're a lucky woman that nothing is broken but that you ain't to have one thing but broth for two days. And no talkin' either so your voice box can heal up. Says you'll probably always have a deeper voice now. The rope came nigh onto . . . well, we ain't goin' to talk about that right now."

Garnet wanted to talk about it. She wanted to rant and rave and jump out of the bed and pitch a royal blue-blooded hissy fit. She wanted to tell Sheriff Gabe Walker that he had skunk's stripes running down his back. That he was a scoundrel of the worst kind and he should be removed from office. He'd accused her falsely. He hadn't protected her

and let those ruffians hang her. He could beg until there
were icicles hanging from the devil's furnace and she
wouldn't forgive him.

Not now. Not ever.

"From that black look on your face, honey, I'm not sure
I want to know what you are thinkin' about," Stella
laughed. "But we'll talk later and maybe you'll be willin'
to change your ways and join us womenfolks of Frenchman's Ford in our sincere efforts to rid this town of the
evils of drink."

Garnet guessed the widow Nash to be about thirty years
old. Big round brown eyes set under dark eyebrows that
looked out of place with all that thick dishwater blonde
hair. Her nose was as straight and classic as the women in
the old paintings and her mouth full, without even the
faintest hint of humor. Stella Nash was no petite little rosebud of a woman. Looking up at her, Garnet figured she
could look Sheriff Gabe right in the eye, which would make
her just under six feet tall, and that wispy waist said that
either Stella had an almighty powerful corset under that
fancy dress or else she'd never had children.

"Don't you go nowhere now, Garnet," Stella waved at
the door and giggled at her own joke.

Garnet propped herself up in the middle of the pillows
and stared at the pale reflection of herself in the mirror
across the room. The mirror was above a dressing table laid
out with a silver brush and comb set and several perfume
bottles. Garnet squinted at the bedraggled mess glaring
back at her and plucked at the ribbons on the nightrail. The
gown was of the finest, softest cotton, robin's egg blue,
trimmed in white ribbons and tiny, little buttons. She
pushed a mop of red, unruly curls back over her shoulders,
but as usual her hair had a mind of its own and slowly
crept back to hang down the front of the gown.

She touched the bandage winding around her neck, not
totally unlike the coil of rope. An achingly cold shiver crept
up her backbone and the results made her head ache even

worse. She heard the scrape of boots coming up the stairs and turned away from the door. Blast it all, her head hurt. She'd been hung and barely escaped death and now she had to face the glorious Sheriff Walker—with a headache. It had to be him coming to tell her that he'd figured out she wasn't guilty after all. She didn't want his apology. She wanted him to go fall flat on his face off the nearest cliff. Or else climb up in that hanging tree and dive bomb right down to the ground on his pretty face.

He muttered under his breath, something about the thing being heavy. She hoped it broke his back, whatever it was. Maybe he'd fall backwards down the stairs and break his fool neck. Not likely, though. He'd probably hit his head and do damage to Stella's floor. Anything as hard as his egotistical-know-it-all head couldn't be harmed with a simple fall down a flight of stairs.

The door flew open and he set her trunk down with a thump in the middle of the floor. A sleeve from her favorite calico dress hung out the side, along with the strings from a bonnet she'd worn all the way across several states. Seemed like she remembered Betsy tidying up that trunk. So why had Sheriff Walker and his pot bellied deputy gone through her things again? He hitched his guns back into a comfortable position and leaned against the door jamb. So the woman was awake and he had to apologize. And apologizing did not come easy for Gabriel Morgan Walker. As a matter of fact, he'd only ever had to eat his words one time before. And they sure hadn't tasted like honey. The bitterness of them still stuck in his craw.

Garnet ignored him. Stella had said the doctor said she couldn't talk. Well, that added to the fact that she wouldn't made for a double determination. He could stand there in those new skin tight jeans, a snowy white shirt and a black leather vest with a big silver star pinned to it, until the devil sat down to tea with the temperance ladies. Tension crackled across the room like the air just before an Arkansas tornado whipped down out of the sky and wreaked havoc.

But she continued to stare at the sun rays drifting lazily through Stella's lace curtains.

"Are you alive?" he finally asked.

She lowered her chin even if it did hurt and glared up at him from under perfectly, naturally arched eyebrows. The chill from her strange blue eyes shot a cold wave through his heart. It was time for the apology and then he'd get out of her room and never look back in that direction again. Not even if he did have to pass the door several times a day when he was on his way to his own room just down the hall.

Just say the words and get back to work, he thought, his strong, square jaw working in as much anger as poured from those frosty eyes. *You'd be upset too if someone had hung you when you were innocent.*

"Well, well," Stella literally flowed into the room.

Garnet turned her head away from Gabe.

Sheriff Walker felt like he'd been dismissed but he hadn't said the words yet and he'd be hung, himself, before he let them lay down there in his soul and fester until another time. He'd made a mistake. One that nearly cost a woman her life and had cost her her voice, no doubt. And he was sure enough man enough to make it right with an apology.

"Good lord," Stella set the tray on the ladderback chair she'd drug over to the bed. "Gabe, for goodness sake, couldn't you have opened the trunk and put her things in proper? Even a fallen lady like Garnet doesn't deserve to have her things slung around like this. I'm ashamed of you. Now get on out of here and go protect Frenchman's Ford. Surely there's a killin' you can take care of. You're not needed here. I can take care of Garnet. Good-bye," she shoved him out the door, not giving him time to say a word before she slammed the door at his back.

She winked at Garnet. "He can sure enough wait a spell before he gets that off his chest. Man made a grave error so we'll let it lay and draw pain for a spell before we allow him to tell you he was wrong. Men are like that, especially those who partake of the devil's fire in the form of liquor. And Gabe Walker might not get fallin' down drunk, but he sure enough provides a place for other men to get it."

A tiny smile twitched at the sides of Garnet's mouth. She could care less if Gabe Walker provided strong drink for the men. She didn't care if he owned every saloon in Frenchman's Ford or if Stella was the head she-coon of the temperance society. Suddenly, Garnet realized that's exactly what Stella was, and shuddered at the idea. That's what she'd been talking about when she said she might convert Garnet to her way of thinking. Good Lord, she'd just fallen out of a hanging tree straight into the bowels of hell. She allowed Stella to slip an oversized white napkin into the collar of the nightrail and feed her a few bites of warm broth as her mind raced around from one horrendous thought to the next. Stella might have put a little ground up fox glove into the broth. In her eyes she'd be thinking that a dead woman would have a better chance at rolling around on puffy white clouds than one who played a piano in a saloon where men actually partook of that vile, evil liquor.

"My husband brought me out here to this forsaken place from the far side of Tennessee. We didn't have children and he wanted an adventure. Adventure killed him and I didn't have a dime left. Just this house, darlin'. Well, town was growing but it didn't have a hotel yet so I just opened up the four extra bedrooms and turned it into a boarding house. Gabe lives here, you know. Right down the hall. He knew I had a spare room so when the doctor said he figured you were going to live, but he didn't know if you'd be right in the head since you might have brain fever, Gabe brought you here. Paid for a week's board and room. Open up your mouth, darlin'. Six bites ain't goin' to get you well. Now where was I? Oh, yes, other boarders come and go and I keep looking for some to stay permanent like, but it makes a living for me. At least until I decide where it is I want to go. I've had a hankerin' to go back East and work harder in the temperance movement but I do hate to leave my dear Joe. He's buried here, you know, and who'd care for his grave if I left? Anyway, Gabe lives here all the time, but I want to get one thing straight right now. Way that man looks at you, I reckon he's goin' to do more than apologize if you'll let him. That's men for you. Either drinkin' or eyein' women. Worthless lot they are. All but my Joe. He was a pure saint. But if you've a mind to let Gabe lead you down the daisy path, then that's your business. It just ain't happenin' in my boarding house. And that's a fact. Ain't got nothing against Gabe Walker. He was good to my husband. Letting him play at being a deputy but that's what killed him. Adventure was what he wanted. But adventure killed him. Mercy, listen to the way I do go on. It's just that I know you played the piano over at the saloon that one night and that Jonah had hired you. And I guess I'm tryin' to make you understand where I stand so you'll know where you're goin' to have to stand to live here."

Garnet tried to get a picture of what Stella was talking about. Maybe she was flitting in and out of consciousness even while she swallowed the tasty broth, because not one thing made a bit of sense. Something about her husband dying and Gabe living there in her boarding house. Faith and saints above as Tavish O'Leary used to say, she'd have to endure him living just down the hallway from her for the next week. That's all she needed! A daily confrontation with the man who'd accused her falsely. Add that on top of a temperance woman who wanted to convert her and she'd be crazier than an outhouse rat by the time she could get out of Frenchman's Ford. The minute she was well she'd be booking passage on a westbound stage. Gussie would be surprised to see her but at least all the weddings would be finished and she wouldn't be forced into marrying a man she didn't know.

The door opened with such force that Stella spilled a

spoonful of soup on the coverlet and Garnet jerked her head around so quickly, it commenced to aching even worse. The sheriff stood there, blocking out most of the light and glaring at the two of them like they were in the midst of robbing a bank.

"I'm not leaving. Not yet. I've come to apologize for making a mistake about you, Garnet Dulan. I should've sent the deputy to check out your story, but I didn't and it nearly cost you your life. I still don't like you and I want you out of my town. So I've paid Stella for a week's room and board and I'll buy you a ticket to anywhere you want to go. Back East where you come from. Out West where you were going, but you're not living in Frenchman's Ford, and that's a fact," Gabe said.

"I'm staying," she whispered, wondering all the time just how she would manage that feat and why she'd made that kind of decision when just moments before she was ready to crawl on her hands and knees out of Frenchman's Ford. Maybe it was the set of his handsome jaw, or the way he thought he could run her life. Well, if he wanted her gone, then she'd be staying in Frenchman's Ford even if she had to scrub floors for Stella and listen to temperance talk from dawn to dusk. But then the simple question burned itself onto her brain. How? If the sheriff wanted her gone then no one would hire her. Without money, she'd be forced to leave.

"No, you ain't," he said, his crystal clear blue eyes little more than slits under heavy dark brows. "Not if I have to carry you kicking and squealing out of my town."

"Drop dead," her voice was barely a raspy mutter.

"I mean it," Gabe said. "That's the end of this discussion. You are leaving in one week. You just decide which way you are going because that's the only decision you get to make, lady."

Garnet shut her eyes and laid her head back on the pillows.

"That won't work," Gabe started across the floor but Stella stopped him midway.

"This is my boarding house, Gabe Walker. You might be the law here in Frenchman's Ford, but honey, I own this house, lock, stock and barrel. That piece of paper you signed when you moved in here said I could kick your sorry rear end out with nothing more than a twenty-four hour notice. Now you better get your hot head on out of here before we both do something we'll regret later. I don't think Jezebel will let you live there permanently and I imagine the towns folks would look down on you living at Jonah's place even if you do own a fourth share of it. If you want this saloon player out of town, then you can run her out, but you're not throwing your weight around in here anymore today. Now, go," she pointed toward the door emphatically.

"Don't you threaten me, Stella," he said.

"Don't make me, Gabe," she said, her nose barely inches from his.

Garnet peeped out one eye and enjoyed the sight immensely. Especially when Sheriff Walker threw up his hands in bewilderment and stomped out into the hall. Every heavy step down the stairs brought a bit more amusement to her eyes.

"Just because he's a man don't mean he can tell me what I can and can't do. Matter of fact, that might be the very thing that makes him worthless—to tell me what I can do. I'm no man's property anymore. Not since Joe died. I own this property whether the government likes it or not. And I don't answer to no man, not even if he's the almighty sheriff," Stella mumbled. "And you might as well open your eyes, girl. I got a few things to say to you, too. You can stay in my house because it's paid up, but you and I ain't going to see eye-to-eye on things either. I'm the president of the local temperance ladies and I don't cotton with no women who play a honky tonk piano in a saloon. I don't expect you'll be playing anywhere in Frenchman's Ford again, but you can just know where I stand. Those dens of evil cause more killin's than an epidemic of cholera. They're nothing but the devil's garden where he plants his seeds. No matter how hard the women work at being good wives, seems like the old devil owns the night, and we mean to stop it. We'll march or we'll fight but we're going to make a decent town out of Frenchman's Ford."

Whew! Garnet didn't have a bit of trouble getting a handle on that. Stella Nash was a temperance queen and Garnet a fallen angel by her standards. A week in the house with her preaching and Garnet would be willing to ride a cross-eyed mule all the way to Bryte, California and marry up with a one-legged, snuff dipping, bald-headed man who lived in a one room dugout infested with rats the size of cotton tail rabbits.

"We understood?" Stella asked.

Garnet nodded.

"Good. Now I might even have you talked into sittin' in a temperance meeting in a couple of nights. Been tryin' for weeks to get the preacher's wife to join us. Just don't seem right somehow for her to stay outside our circle. She's the backbone of the religious community. You'd think she would see how important it is that we take care of these cesspools of sin."

Sure, I understand. I'll be running out of town dragging that trunk behind me, begging the Paiute Indians to scalp me before I sit in on one of your holier-than-thou meetings, lady, Garnet thought. But rather than mumble a word, she fluttered her eyes a few times and faked sleep. Lord, Almighty, but what had she gotten herself into? Hanging sounded good compared to a week in the house with Stella Nash preaching temperance, and Gabe Walker demanding that she leave his desert haven.

Gabe marched into the saloon, slammed his hat down on the bar and bristled when Jonah raised an eyebrow in his direction. He'd been angry in his lifetime but nothing compared to the rage right then.

"Tea?" Jonah asked.

Gabe nodded and Jonah reached under the counter for a fresh pitcher of sweet tea. He filled a glass to the brim and set it before Gabe. "She awake?" He asked.

Gabe nodded again, not trusting his voice to do anything but scream and rant.

"Honest mistake," Jonah said. "You apologize yet?"

Gabe nodded a third time.

"Well, that's probably going to take more than a glass of sugared-up tea to get the taste out of your mouth, old friend," Jonah said. "You might change your views on drinkin' the strong stuff before you get that business swallowed."

"She's leaving town in one week. I don't care if she goes West or East, or I have to sell her to the Indians as a white slave. She's nothing but trouble and she's leaving," Gabe said.

"Don't see how you can do that legally. If she's not breaking no laws, you can't make her do one thing," Jonah said. "Women might get up in arms about you forcin' her out of town. Lord knows we got few enough women as it is. Just last night all four of my girls had at least a dozen proposals. I think Emmy might even be thinkin' serious on one of them. Silver miner declared she was his good luck at the card tables and said he'd be back tonight."

Gabe didn't want to talk about Jonah's girls. He didn't want to discuss anything. He just wanted his life back the way it was before he walked into the saloon three nights before and found the drop-down-dead-gorgeous-red-haired woman playing the piano. He didn't like being wrong, and he sure didn't like having to admit it. He glared at Jonah through the amber liquid in the glass.

"I don't care if it's legal or not. Women got no rights in Nevada Territory. They might be able to own property up north in Oregon, but not here, and I can run her out of town if I want to," Gabe declared, a bit hoarsely.

"Well, you better do it quietly if you want to keep that star on your chest," Jonah said. " 'Course I could use a hand here in the bar. You don't have to be a sheriff, you know. And Zebediah could use you at the silver mines any day of the week. And what's that about women ownin' property? I do believe the Widow Nash owns that house down the street. Husband left it to her lock, stock and barrel and paid for at that. So what're you going to do if Garnet decides to buy a place in Frenchman's Ford? She could argue that if the widow can own property, then she can too."

The muscles in Gabe's jaw tightened and his full mouth became little more than a thin line. The thunder flowing from his eyes could almost be heard bouncing around in the empty saloon. "I'll keep this badge and I'll clean this town up to be a decent place to live for families and children. And Garnet Dulan will be gone in seven days. You can drag out the stone and chisel and write it down for the whole town to see."

"Anything you say," Jonah nodded in assent.

He turned his back to hide the grin. There had never been a woman capable of making his best friend that mad, and Jonah would bet his seventy five percent of the saloon that in a week's time, Garnet Dulan was still in Frenchman's Ford.

Gabe finished the tea in one loud gulp and stormed out, as mad as he'd been when he came in. Dust rolled up half way to his knees as he stomped across the street, dodging a wagon load of children with their mother and father. They waved and yelled at him, but he didn't take time to stop and visit with them. He threw open the door of the jailhouse and slung his black hat toward the peg on the wall. It missed and hit the floor. He kicked it across the room and plopped down in the chair behind his desk.

"Sheriff?" His deputy, Les, came through the back door. "Guess the prisoner is going to live?"

"Don't talk to me about it," Gabe said. "Don't even mention her name and don't ask any questions. She's leaving town in a week, and I don't ever want to hear another word about her."

"Yes, sir," the deputy nodded seriously. "Where's she goin'?"

Gabe slung his chair back with enough force that it hit the floor in a dull thud. He retrieved his hat and slammed it down on his head and was out the door before the deputy could say another word.

"Hey, Sheriff," Dusty, the general store owner called out. "I hear the woman you had in custody, the one that got hanged, is going to live. Don't that beat all?"

Gabe pretended he didn't hear the man and kept walking. One week. Seven days. The talk would die down when she was gone. And gone she would be, if he really did have to sell her to the Piaute Indians.

Chapter Five

Three men sat at the breakfast table the next morning with Garnet. Stella had all but thrown a fit when she found Garnet sitting in the living room when she came down to prepare breakfast for her boarders, but Garnet whispered that she had no intentions of lying in bed for a whole week. Stella had snorted but she went on into the kitchen and Garnet had to smile when she heard her slamming pots and pans around, followed by the sound of muttering and mumbling. So the Widow Nash didn't like her authority to be usurped either. Perhaps she and Sheriff Gabe Walker should get together. That would create a big enough clash to knock Frenchman's Ford all the way off the map and most likely kill them both before they'd been married a whole day.

Now she sat across the long table from three men—the sheriff, who looked like he could chew shoe leather; a middle aged salesman who said he was just in Frenchman's Ford for the one night, and a newspaper man who was going to Sacramento, California to write a story about the women who'd braved all the elements to go to California to marry the gold miners there.

"Well, Garnet here is one of those women. Except she decided she didn't want to marry up with a man she didn't

48

know after all and she stopped here in Frenchman's Ford but she'll be goin' on here in a few days so you'll probably run into her in California if she was to decide to go that way," Stella said, replenishing the basket of hot biscuits in the middle of the table.

"Is that true?" The newspaper man eyed her curiously.

She nodded.

"Do you think those women will really go through with the marriages?" he asked.

She nodded again.

"Do you ever talk?"

"I can't talk much," she whispered.

"Hung," the other man said. "I heard at the saloon last night about her. She played the piano at the Silver Dollar for one night and then she got arrested for bank robbery and murder. The real culprits come into town and broke her out of jail, hung her and took off south when the sheriff arrived on the scene. They figured she was dead but she survived it and that's what that bandage is around her neck."

Well, thank you so much, Garnet thought, her blue eyes nothing but slits as she glared at the man.

"Want to give me a story about that?" The newspaper man was suddenly very interested in the tall red-haired woman sharing the table with them.

She shook her head and noticed at the same time that Gabe looked a bit pale. If for no other reason than to make Gabe squirm she should give the man his story. But she didn't like the fellow one whit better than she did the sheriff.

"Well, the brides on that wagon train will be in for a surprise right off the bat," the man said, puffing out his chest a bit with information. "You see, they think they're going to a town named Bryte. That's what the wagon masters thought when they left California last year and went to St. Joseph, Missouri to round up the brides. I can't imagine what kind of women would sign on for a trip like that," he eyed Garnet, who shot daggers at him with her blue eyes. He dropped his gaze and went on, "Anyway, the miners had a deal going with some fellow named Bryte who was going to sell each of them some land and they'd name their newfound town after him. Only the deal went sour and they've bought land in and around a little town not far from there named Washington. Some of them have acreage outside of town where they can have little truck farms; some of them had houses raised right in town. But those girls aren't going to the bright star out in the promised land. They're just going to plain old Washington."

"Mail?" Garnet whispered. "My sisters will send mail to Bryte."

"Oh, it'll go on to Washington. Everyone in that area is lookin' for those wagons to come pulling in," he said.

"I see," she said. "Excuse me. Keep your seats," she said as they laid their napkins down and prepared to stand. "Have a nice day." She was halfway up the stairs when she heard Gabe's boots on the steps behind her. She moved to one side of the wide staircase to let him pass her by, but he made no effort to go faster. When they reached the top of the stairs, he brushed past her, his arm touching hers briefly. Sparks ignited off the tension between them and crackled in the hallway outside her bedroom.

"Thanks for not giving him that story. It could have made me look pretty stupid," he said.

"You are stupid," she said.

He gritted his teeth and stormed on down the hall to his bedroom where he slammed the door shut with enough force to rattle the pictures on the walls. *That woman has to be gone in a week.* He'd be stark raving mad if she wasn't.

Garnet opened her trunk and retrieved a shawl and her best straw hat. She'd take a morning stroll up and down the main street of town and have a look around to see if there might be a place she could work. Jonah probably wouldn't think of hiring her again. At least that's what he'd said that morning they hauled her off to the jail. That he couldn't afford to have his place shot up by those who'd wonder if she was guilty or innocent. But surely there were other places where she could work and make enough money to stay alive for a while in Frenchman's Ford. Even if it was only a month or two. At least she would have proven that the sheriff couldn't run her out of town, and her pride would be intact.

She threw the deep blue shawl around her shoulders and stepped out of the room just as Gabe in all his sheriff's finery opened his door down the hall. The black leather vest was only a symbol of the fury surrounding him like a shroud. The sparkling silver star pinned to it looked almost tarnished when she thought of the way she hadn't played right into his little plan to ship her out of his town. His hat sat on his handsome head off at a rakish angle, showing her and the world that he was still in control . . . or thought he was. He tipped his hat in her direction and with a ramrod straight back, waited for her to precede him down the stairs.

"Thank you," she said, holding on to the banister for support. Faith and saints, there had never been a man who'd affected her like this. It had to be the collision of their stubborn wills that made her knees go weak when he was in her presence. Well, next week when she wasn't on that stage leaving town, her jelly-filled legs would have steel in them, because she would have proven to him and herself both that he wasn't near tough enough to tell Garnet Diana Dulan what to do.

Like a gentleman he held the front door open for her. The bright morning sun beamed down on her face and she didn't even care that she might get a freckle. Not that morning. She inhaled deeply and started off down the street with high spirits. Today she would find a job that would pay enough to keep her in a room at the Nash boarding house for a while longer. Frenchman's Ford was a growing town and there would be something Garnet could do. She refused to touch the money in the bottom of the trunk; not unless worse came to worst. That was her entire savings and when it was gone she truly wouldn't have a say-so in her future. Besides, if she didn't take the sheriff's offer to leave town in a week when her room and board played out, then he most likely wouldn't offer again, and she'd be stranded for sure. No money. No way out.

Today had to be her lucky day. She strolled all the way to the end of the street, bypassing the Silver Dollar, yearning to go inside and play the piano for just a little while. Just to hear the melody floating around in the empty saloon even if she could never play there again. If the town were bigger, say the size of Little Rock, Arkansas with lots of women and children, she might put out a shingle and give music lessons. She remembered the lady who gave lessons to her cousin, Dora, back in Arkansas. Garnet had been living with an uncle in those days, when she was eight years old and had already been shifted amongst the relatives several times. Dora hated practicing her lessons, but Garnet had taken to music, holding on to it like it was a lifeline. She and Dora made it up between them that Garnet would practice for her. Dora's mother was always busy with other things and kept the door to the parlor shut, so on lesson day, Dora showed Garnet what the teacher had taught her, and the rest of the week, she and Dora would disappear into the parlor for an hour a day and she'd practice.

She passed a lumber business but there wasn't a bit of sense in going in there. She crossed the street and looked at the Spur Saloon with the idea of just stepping up to the bar and asking for a job, but it seemed useless since the owner there would bear the same feelings as Jonah did. He wouldn't be willing to hire the notorious Garnet Dulan, the only woman who'd most likely ever been inside the Frenchman's Ford jail.

When she reached the general store she realized that Gabe was only a few feet behind her, keeping his distance yet following her all the same. She gritted her teeth and opened the door. There was no reason for him to watch her like that, other than just to plain make her angry and convince her to leave town. Was he going to shirk his duties the whole week in order to keep her in his sights? Now, just what kind of sheriff was that?

"Mornin' ma'am," the proprietor of the store grinned. "You that Garnet Dulan that got hanged, ain't you?"

She nodded, tired of bobbing her head up and down, but not trusting her injured voice box to do much talking. She fingered the bolts of fabric, lingering over a lovely emerald green satin and thinking of Emmy wearing a saloon girl's dress made from it. The door opened and she turned at the same time the store owner did.

"Well, mornin' Sheriff," he said.

"And a good mornin' to you, Dusty," Gabe said, his eyes never leaving Garnet.

"Why are you following me?" Garnet asked.

"Because I intend to make sure that you are just out for a little morning exercise and not trying to talk any of the good citizens of Frenchman's Ford into giving you employment. Because I fully well intend that you are leaving this town at the end of a week minus one day. That should give you time to heal and your rent will be up by then," he said without blinking or backing up a step from the red-haired beauty standing so close to him that he could have fallen into those lovely blue eyes for a lifetime.

"She didn't ask me for a job," Dusty said. "But if she had, I would have had to turn her down. Town ain't big enough for me to be hiring help. Now if she was willin' to marry me, I might think on that."

Garnet jerked her head around to give him a "drop dead" look. Dusty was bald headed and had little beady eyes that looked at her like he was undressing her right there in the store. Was she willing to marry a sleazy man like him just to win the argument with Sheriff Walker? She didn't think so. Her skin crawled at the idea of marrying the man. No, she'd let the sheriff sell her to the Indians like he'd threatened first. She'd made up her mind not to go on to California and marry a man whose name she'd pull out of a hat. She'd rather be hanged again than let herself be talked into the same predicament right here in Nevada Territory.

"Well, I was just making sure she didn't come in here and ask for a job," Gabe said. "She can spend the whole day in this place looking at fancy material but don't you be hiring or marrying her. We want decent women in Frenchman's Ford, Dusty. You can order you one of them mail-order brides from back East if you've a mind to marry."

Dusty laughed. "Now why would I do that? You're going to clean up the town in a few months and there'll be a whole swarm of women coming to town. Young ones who'll think it's a real honor to be marryin' up with the man who owns the biggest general store in the whole territory."

Gabe grinned. He would have sworn on his mother's Bible that Garnet's bubble had burst when he swung open the door. Well, she might as well face the facts. She was leaving town, and he was winning the battle. That was all there was to it. She nodded politely at the storekeeper and Gabe opened the door for her, resituated the broad brimmed black hat on his head and felt better than he had in days.

"I'm not so stupid any more, am I?" he asked softly as he fell into step beside her.

"Worse?" she said.

"And how could that be?" He asked.

"Jezebel," she said softly.

"You wouldn't dare," he said, his skin crawling. Mercy, he'd been trying for weeks to figure out a way to clean up Jezebel's Palace. It was located on the outskirts of town and the woman kept her distance from the sheriff. The few decent women in town avoided her like the plague, but the men kept her business booming.

Garnet picked up the pace and stopped across the street from the boarding house at the small church. The doors were open so she went inside. The sheriff chuckled and mumbled something about there surely not being a job inside there for her as he turned around and went back to the jail.

The church was small, only six short pews on each side of the building with a center aisle. A small pulpit in the front with a rough hewn deacon's bench behind where the preacher must stand to deliver his sermons. A piano off to one side and three small pews on the other where the choir must sit on Sunday morning. She went to the first pew on the left and sat down. Total silence and peace surrounded her.

Lord, she prayed silently, *please help me. I don't know if I'm supposed to stay here in Frenchman's Ford. If I'm not then close the doors and I'll go on to California even though I don't want to. But if I am supposed to be here, then open up something for me. I'll swallow my pride if I can't stay but don't let that mean sheriff win just because he's a man.*

"Garnet?" Betsy touched her shoulder.

Garnet jumped two inches off the pew then settled back down, her heart pounding in her chest. Mercy, but she thought the Lord, himself, had just touched her there for a moment.

"I'm so sorry I scared you," Betsy said. "I'd heard about what happened to you and was just surprised to see you, that's all. Couldn't mistake that red hair though. Had to be you."

"Hello," Garnet managed to say.

"Whew, you sure did lose your voice didn't you?" Betsy said.

Garnet bobbed her head.

"Sheriff says all over town that you're leaving in a few days," Betsy said.

Garnet shook her head. "Not if I can find some way to keep my body and soul together."

"Well, we'll have to see about that, won't we?" Betsy

patted her back as she slid into the pew beside her. "Never know what might come up here in the next week. Me, I think Sheriff Walker is overstepping his boundaries by forcing you out of town. It was his stupid mistake, not yours, that caused you to be hung in the first place."

"Thank you," Garnet said.

"How are you getting along with Stella Nash? Now there's a woman to be careful about. She's into this temperance stuff so deep it's become her god. Matthew says it's all right to protest when you feel like you got a cause. I'm against liquor but I'm also against a woman acting like she does. Then she tries to make me join her group and all it does is make me balk at it even more," Betsy said.

"What, Momma? What does that woman try to make you do?" A little red-haired girl asked from behind the pulpit where she'd been dusting.

"That's not for you to know, Charity. Come here and meet Garnet Dulan. She might be staying with us here in Frenchman's Ford," Betsy said.

"Do I have to give up my bed for her?" Charity asked.

"That's not very nice," Betsy said. "I didn't mean she was going to live with us, but rather that she might be living in our town."

"I'm Charity and I think I might like you," the girl stuck out her hand.

Garnet smiled as she shook hands with the child. "Thank you," she said.

"What happened to your voice? Is that because they hung you up in the tree and then cut you down before you was full dead? What did it feel like to be nearly dead? Did it hurt?" Charity asked, her eyes big with questions.

"Charity Ruth!" her mother chastised.

"All right," Garnet patted Betsy's hand. "Can't talk right now, but when my voice comes back I'll tell you about it."

"Fair enough," Charity said. "I got everything ready for next Sunday, Momma. Can I go on back home now and work on my reading?"

"Yes, but you aren't the boss of your brothers, so don't you be making them sit up and play school with you," Betsy said. "Tell your Dad that I'll be along soon, then he can go out to the Flashers and check on the new baby."

"Okay, Momma. Nice to meet you Miss Garnet. Get well soon so you can tell me all about that hanging stuff," Charity threw back over her shoulder as she ran out the doors.

"Lovely child," Garnet said.

"Yes, but I'm afraid the world is in for a surprise. She'll run Susan B. Anthony some competition when she's grown. Says she's going to be a doctor or a lawyer. Mercy, I don't know some days how I birthed a daughter so outspoken," Betsy said.

"Good girl," Garnet said. "Thanks for talking to me. I'm going back to the boarding house now. If you hear of anything let me know." The last few words were mouthed with no sound.

"I'll do it. You take care of yourself this week," Betsy said.

"Find a job in the church?" Gabe asked her when she opened the door to the boarding house. He sat in the living room with a newspaper propped up in front of his face and his feet propped on a hassock covered with a peacock done up in needlepoint.

She nodded and he frowned.

"You are leaving in six days." The thunder was back in his blue eyes.

Well, so he's got some noise hiding behind those pretty blue eyes this morning. Don't he know that thunder is just noise?

"And what are you going to do? Preach without a voice?" he asked bluntly.

"They're going to pay me to pray for your wayward soul," she managed to get out before her voice stopped.

"Don't push me, Garnet," he declared coldly.

She simply smiled sweetly and went upstairs where she paced the floor until the little tinkling crystal bell announced that lunch was ready. Sitting across the table from him was a pure cross to bear but she managed to swallow a few bites of the broth Stella put before her, more out of spite than hunger.

For the next five days she fell into a routine. She ate breakfast, went for her walks with Gabe Walker following a short distance behind her, paced the floor until lunch worrying about what on earth she was going to do, took an afternoon nap and then went back down to supper. By the end of the week she was eating solid foods but her voice was still hoarse and disappeared completely after a few words.

On the fifth night she left the dinner table and Gabe followed her. "So which way is it to be day after tomorrow? East? West? Which way are you going, Garnet? You know you've lost because there is no place in town for the likes of you, so make up your mind." He pointed his finger at her and talked down to her, doing nothing more than making her so mad she could have bitten the finger off and had it for dessert.

"It ain't over yet," she said, slapping his hand aside and wondering what caused her hand to burn when it touched him.

He jumped as if he'd been struck by lightning. His bare hand burned where she'd touched him. He looked down at it to see if she might have actually set his shirt sleeve afire. "Like I told you before, don't push me. I'm not a mean person, but I said you were leaving town and you will. This is going to be a decent town for decent people. I don't want a sideshow made out of the woman who survived the hanging."

"Drop dead," she said, ignoring her shaking hands as she used the banister for support and started to her room.

"You've said that before. Saying it don't make it. I'm not going away. This town wants me to stay here," he said.

"Town doesn't want me to go. You do," she turned back from half way up and glared at him.

"That's right. The town doesn't know how to take care of itself. That's why they hired me, Garnet. And I will see you on a stage day after tomorrow morning. So you better be thinking about where you are going," he said forcefully.

She snorted slightly and let him have his day. There was still twenty four hours plus a night. She wasn't whipped yet even if she was about ready to chose the westbound stage. By the time she got to her room she was ready to kick holes in the walls, throw the silver hair brush at the mirror, or slice the quilt into ribbons with her sewing scissors. Anything to vent out some of the rage in her heart.

She undressed, carefully draping her dress over the back of the rocker and slipped her worn nightrail over her head. She had money. She could stay just to spite him. Even if it was only for another week. Stella would rent her the room. She knew it, but she'd prayed and asked God for help. If the help didn't come by the time the westbound train left Frenchman's Ford day after tomorrow morning, she'd have to be on it.

Whether she liked it or not.

She lay down on her bed, pulling the covers up around her neck. The night air had turned cool. Fall wasn't far away now, and winter would be nipping close behind it. But even the snows of winter couldn't compare to the coldness in Garnet's usually warm heart. She shut her eyes and tried to will herself to sleep. It was impossible. All she could see was the glint in Gabe's eyes when he told her she definitely would be leaving on that stage.

Chapter Six

The setting sun put on quite a radiant show for Garnet as she watched the ending day from the window of the Widow Nash's boarding house. She drew her shawl tightly around her shoulders and touched the bandage on her neck. The skin had begun to heal quite nicely, leaving behind a nasty red welt so she'd kept it covered a while longer. Somehow it made it more bearable to her. There'd always be a scar there, but she was indeed a lucky woman to be alive to see it each day. She paced the floor for ten minutes and then slung her shawl over the back of the rocking chair beside the bed. Her neck was marred; she still couldn't speak above a hoarse whisper. But her spirit hadn't died when they chased that horse out from under her. Her ribs still ached where that fool man had kicked her and the big bruise on her cheek was every color in the rainbow, but her feet still worked, and she was free. She could walk out of that room and down the street if she wanted to do so. She had one more day to figure out whether or not she could stay in Frenchman's Ford. One more day. It didn't look good, but then it hadn't looked good when that horse left her hanging in a tree either and she'd survived that. So who was to say something still couldn't come up?

Yes, and horses and cows might someday sprout wings

and fly like sparrows, she told herself. It looked like the good sheriff was going to ship her out no matter what.

She opened up the trunk and took out her best blue dress. The collar wasn't so tight as to put pressure on the bandage. She shook the wrinkles from it as best she could and gathered up her drawers and corset. She'd get dressed and take a walk in the evening air. She shouldn't spend her last night in Frenchman's Ford watching life go on from her window. She should be out there taking a stroll.

Maybe something would come to her, an idea of just how she planned to keep her body and soul together. This situation wasn't totally unlike the one in St. Joseph, Missouri back in the spring. Jake was dead. The will had been read and the Dulan sisters had a room for one week. After that they were on their own. They'd coerced Hank into letting them join the wagon train of mail order brides and they'd had each other. Now Garnet Dulan had to stand alone. Gussie was on her way to California to marry some unsuspecting poor soul who thought he was getting a sweet little wife. Garnet smiled. Whoever got Gussie for a wife had better keep his britches on twenty four hours a day because if he didn't that Dulan sister would be wearing them.

No, Garnet didn't have her four sisters for support in this decision, but she was as brave and stubborn as the rest of them, and she could darn well make up her own mind as to what she intended to do with her life. And she was going to step right out into the night air and have a little walk to clear her mind. Glad that she had one corset with front laces, she shimmied into it and her underwear. When she drew the laces tight against aching ribs, she sucked in air and a fine bead of sweat popped out under her nose. She fought down a wave of nausea and didn't draw up the corset as tight as she usually did.

When she had herself fully dressed and the shawl wrapped back around her shoulders, she opened the door. Not even the Widow Nash was going to keep her in this room another minute. The final countdown had arrived. She had to figure something out by the time she went to bed tonight or else tell Gabe to buy her a ticket west tomorrow morning. She swallowed hard and gingerly put one foot out into the hallway. From there, it wasn't nearly so hard. She didn't encounter Stella Nash in the living room when she descended the wide staircase, nor did she see the sheriff when she let herself out the door and inhaled deeply of the night air.

She turned right and strolled down the wooden sidewalk slowly past the bank situated between the boarding house and the Silver Dollar Saloon. The banker had coldly turned her down the day before when she approached him for a job. No, ma'am, he would not hire a woman who had the faintest smell of indiscretion on her. Not even if she was innocent. Smoke rolled out the swinging doors of the saloon followed by laughter and a few women's giggles. Business as usual. But with no piano player. On a whim, she swung open the doors and marched up to the bar. Gabe Walker leaned against one end and a hot flush filled her cheeks when she caught him staring at her. He was a pure bred buzzard, she kept telling herself as she crossed the room. With him standing there like some guardian devil, Jonah sure enough wouldn't reconsider and hire her back, but she had to try or she'd never forgive herself.

"Miss Garnet," Jonah tipped his head toward her. "You ain't left town yet. I thought Gabe said in a week. Guess it has only been . . ." He couldn't finish the sentence. Those cool blue eyes, the bandage wrapped around her neck and the set of her jaw chilled his soul.

"I still need a job," she said.

"No, you don't," Sheriff Walker said right beside her. "You are healed enough to get out of Frenchman's Ford, and you are leaving tomorrow morning."

"Jonah?" Garnet whispered. "I was innocent."

"Don't matter," Jonah said. "For one thing the good sheriff here owns a fourth of this establishment. For another, like I told you that morning, innocent or guilty could be a problem. Some men would say you were one; some another and the fights would ruin my saloon. So the answer is no."

"I see," Garnet said. She trilled her fingers across the piano keys as she left the saloon. A sudden silence filled the whole room as the patrons got ready for entertainment. They were as disappointed as Garnet when she left without even one farewell song. She'd loved playing the fast songs; loved the way it livened up a room full of cigar smoking men. But evidently those days were over, and now she had to figure out something else.

She reached the end of the sidewalk and crossed the dusty, dirty street to the other side. Laughter and the deep, resonant timbre of men's voices floated out of The Spur in the night air. Jonah's competition. Would they need a piano player? She opened the heavy wooden door and marched inside. Silence as deafening as what she'd just left at the Silver Dollar cut through the room like a sharp knife.

"Who you lookin' for?" the skinny bartender asked before she reached the bar.

"Not who? What?" she said, taking in the whole place with one sweeping glance. No piano. Of course, that could be rectified if the owner was willing to purchase one and give her a job. The Spur wasn't much more than a dirty, dark building with a couple of barrels topped off with a wide board for a bar. No pretty mirror. No piano. No shiny glasses sitting in a row.

"What are you lookin' for then? You one of them temperance women?" the barkeep asked.

"She's the one they hanged for that murder," one man said from the end of the bar. "She's been proved not guilty."

"I'm looking for a job. I'm a piano player," Garnet said.

"Well, you ain't playin' in here. For one thing we ain't got a piano and another, I wouldn't hire you. Woman's place is in the home. Cookin' and cleanin' and makin' babies. You want to play a piano you go to church of a Sunday. Lots of good men in Frenchman's Ford lookin' for a good wife. Wouldn't care if you got a hangman's scar on your neck. So get on out of here, woman."

Garnet nodded slightly. She'd tried. She'd failed. But that didn't mean she was beaten. Not yet, anyway. She still had until morning.

"Come on, I'll walk you back to the boarding house," Sheriff Walker took her arm when she was back out on the sidewalk.

The touch of his fingers on her elbow drove a wave of heat through her so warm that she flushed. She slapped his hand away, her fingers touching his and bringing on more heat. "Don't touch me," she whispered.

"Give it up," he said. "You are not wanted in Frenchman's Ford, Garnet Dulan. Don't be stubborn. We want good wholesome women here, not your kind."

"Why don't you run Jonah's girls out of town or shut down Jezebel's place?" she said, the last words barely audible.

Gabe threw back his head and laughed. "You got nerve woman. I'll give you that. You surely got nerve."

She stopped at the general store and stared in the window, ignoring him as much as possible as he crossed the street and went into the boarding house. An array of items caught her eye. A pail for milking, a pale blue dress sprinkled with light yellow flowers, a sewing machine. Things a decent woman would want. Not something a piano player needed.

Her eyes took in the newest in sewing machines. She'd used one just like that in Arkansas when she made the yellow satin dress. It had belonged to all the girls at the saloon. They'd pooled their money and bought it for Garnet and Daisy to sew dresses for all of them. Too bad there wasn't a call for fancy dresses in Frenchman's Ford. She might eke out a living for a few months making them.

"Miss Garnet?" a timid voice said beside her, causing her to jump and the corset to dig into that painful place in her ribs.

"Emmy?" Garnet looked the woman in the eye. A tall beauty with dark hair and deep brown eyes.

"Jonah said I could have a few minutes break to talk to you. I been wantin' to come to the boarding house all week but the Widow Nash would most likely kick me out in the street. She's one of them temperance women you know. Come here from back East and her poor, poor old husband couldn't do a thing with her. He was about twenty years older'n her and he probably never knew a moment's peace until he died," she said.

Garnet had to agree even if she didn't say a word.

"Anyway, I been wantin' to talk to you ever since they hauled you off to jail. It's just I didn't know how to ask. You see, I want that yellow dress and that hat thing with the feathers of yours. We're about of a size and I want it so bad. Wanted it from the first time I laid eyes on it when you come waltzin' down them stairs. I've got money saved up and I'll be more than glad to buy it from you. We can't find things like that in the Frenchman's Ford general store."

Garnet grinned. So her walk in the evening air had been profitable after all.

"Anyway, you set a fair price and I won't even argue, if you'd be willing to part with it. And the other girls want to know where it is that you buy things like that. Goldie and Pansy and Rosy all want one. We had a mind to wait until six o'clock ever evening and then come parading down the stairs kind of like you did. One at a time. Kind of tease the menfolks with it so they'd be more free with their money," Emmy said.

Garnet nodded. That sewing machine had a price tag of ten dollars hanging on it. Garnet had just found a job. It might not involve playing a piano in the evenings and sleeping until noon every day, but it would put money in her pocket.

"Come home with me and we'll get it," Garnet said so softly that Emmy strained to hear her.

"Oh, no," Emmy said. "I couldn't. Jonah said five

minutes and no more. And the Widow Nash scares the devil
right out of me. You bring it along sometime tomorrow to
the saloon and we'll make the deal then. And thank you,
Miss Garnet. I'm right sorry things didn't work out for you
at the Silver Dollar, but I'm so tickled to have that dress I
could just jump up and down."

There was a new spring in her step when she opened the
front door to the boarding house. Sheriff Walker was
sprawled out in a chair with a glass of tea in one hand and
a newspaper in the other. She felt his eyes on her but tried
her best to pretend he wasn't anything more than a piece
of furniture. She nodded at Stella, sitting as upright as a
sober judge on Sunday morning on the front pew of church.
Stella had a bit of embroidery in her hands and her mouth
was set so firm that Garnet wondered if she might crack
her face if she smiled.

"You've got a guest," Stella said abruptly. "The
preacher's wife. She said she'd wait in your room. I tried
to get her to sit with us but she'd have no part of it. Guess
she's afraid I might talk her into joining the Temperance
Society. Ask me, it ought to be a law made against the
preacher's wife not joining."

Garnet nodded slightly and hurried up the stairs. Stella
Nash was surely a piece of work. The temperance ladies
were fighting for more than just abolition of liquor in public
places. They were also battling for women's rights. And a
woman had a right to join or not to join as they saw fit.
Preacher's wife or not.

Betsy was sitting in the rocking chair when she opened
the door. "Good evening, Garnet. Oh, don't try to be talking, honey. I know your voice box is still damaged and you
can't do no more than whisper. So I'll do the talkin'. Take
off your shawl and sit a spell with me. It's so peaceful and
quiet up here. Some days with three kids and a preacher
husband, I just crave a little peace and quiet. Today has
been one of them. I told you I'd hunt around and see if
there was anything you might do or such so you could stay

in Frenchman's Ford. I'm not one to sit still and wait for things to come about, so I've been out helpin' take care of things for you. Wasn't right that Gabe locked you up when it wouldn't have took nothing but a couple of hours to check out your story. And it sure wasn't right that that lazy deputy of his let them kidnap you out of the jail. I've come on behalf of the ladies of the church to apologize for the way the town has treated you and to put something before you that might help you stay around."

Garnet listened and gently nodded her head a couple of times to let Betsy know she was hearing every word. "Thank you," she mouthed but not much sound came out.

"Oh, no thanks are necessary. I know you can't be playin' the piano in the saloons no more because of what has happened. I watched you go in the Silver Dollar and come out again, and you was gone for a while so I expect you went into the Spur, too. They ain't goin' to hire you, Garnet. We'd like to offer you the teacher's job but you can't talk for a long time if ever, so that's out of the question, but I for one and the other ladies in the church want you to know we're trying to figure something out," Betsy said.

"I'm going to sew," Garnet said very low. She opened her trunk and took out the yellow dress, draped it over the bed, along with the black stockings and head piece. "For Jonah's women. Sold this tonight."

"It's beautiful," Betsy fingered the black lace and satin fabric. "You made this?"

Garnet nodded and sat down on the bed.

"Well, there's sure enough a place for you in Frenchman's Ford then," Betsy smiled beautifully, her light brown eyes twinkling. "Yes, sir, I liked you the first time I brought you food in the jail. Women folks in Frenchman's Ford will keep you so busy you'll have to turn down work."

"Even if I make this kind of thing?" Garnet asked.

"Oh they won't care who for all you sew for, long as they get something done," Betsy said. "And now, what I come to visit you for wasn't just to sit in the quiet of your room and look outside without a trio of younguns screamin' and hollerin' at me. It was to tell you that I went over to visit with Zebediah Jones this afternoon. When God called us from West Virginia to bring the gospel to the Frontier, we just up and come out here. Zebediah is an old silver miner who's richer than Midas and he was in town the day our stage coach stopped here. We was really thinkin' of goin' to California when we left the East. Anyway, he saw us bone-weary and hungry climbin' out of that stage and asked us where we was headed and why was we draggin' three little children around in the desert? So we told him what we was about and he said wasn't no place in the world needed a preacher more than Frenchman's Ford and he'd give us a place to stay if we'd preach in the church he'd already built. We talked it over and decided that God was givin' us an opportunity. Zebediah had us a bigger house built with a nice loft sectioned off with one side for Charity and the other for the two boys. But until he got all that done, we lived in a tiny little cabin back in behind the church. It's only got one room and a mighty small loft. Anyway, I went to see him today and he says you are right welcome to the cabin for as long as you want it. Only rent he'll take is that you show up at the church on Sunday mornin's and play the piano for us. We been prayin' for months that God would send us somebody to play for us, and He's answered our prayers, even if it wasn't just like we figured He'd do."

Garnet stared at her for a full three minutes, purely stupefied. Surely there was a catch somewhere. "Are you sure?" she asked, drawing her eyebrows down from a bed of wrinkles in her forehead.

"Sure am. I was frettin' about how you'd make a livin' and all. And whether you could be content to live in town. The cabin is right up behind the church, just past the cemetery which lies back of the church. Kind of a pretty little place. Got a well, a pump in the kitchen side of the room, a bed with a feather mattress. I left it there when we moved into the big parsonage in case we ever needed to use the place for company. You'd have to find some sheets and a few things to cook with. Like I said, it's just a little old cabin. Zebediah built it for himself but he found out he didn't like town all the time so he put him up another one up by his silver mine. Says he's content up there. Anyway it's plenty big for one woman who's a mind to sew pretty dresses."

"When?" Garnet mouthed.

"Tomorrow morning right early I'll send Matthew around to carry your trunk down there. He's going to bring the wagon to the general store anyway. Got to get a bag of corn for the chickens, so he'll be coming right past here and going right past the little cabin on his way back home since we live on down the road closer to the river," Betsy said.

"Could he bring a sewing machine for me, too?" Garnet asked.

"Sure, he could. That one in the window at the general store? It's expensive, Garnet. Ten whole dollars. You got that much?" Betsy asked.

"Got that much. I'll go first thing in the morning and get a few things, if Matthew doesn't mind," she said, her voice getting hoarser with every word.

"No more talkin' now. You done already overdone it. I'm goin' to leave now. You just make it through one more night in this house," Betsy shuddered and giggled in mock horror. "And we'll get you out of it in the mornin'. I swear if you'd a had to stay much longer, Stella would have had you crazy or else takin' the oath."

Garnet grinned. *You got that right, sister*, she thought and waved as Betsy slipped out the door. She watched her all the way down the stairs and listened when Stella offered her a bit of hot tea before she left. Betsy declined, saying that she must get home to read her children a bedtime story before they went to sleep. Sheriff Walker barely spoke.

Mercy, but he was going to have an attack of acute apo-plexy tomorrow morning. He'd insisted that she would be on a stage going anyway out of Frenchman's Ford she wanted to go, and now he was going to have to sit in church and listen to her play a religious piano for the congregation. That was going to sit in his egotistical craw like a mouth full of bitter herbs.

Garnet eased the door shut. Now wasn't life a mysterious work of art. Last night she'd been all worried about whether she should really go to California and impose on Gussie, of if she should go east and ask Gypsy Rose to put her up for the winter months. Tonight she had a job in mind and a place to live while she did it. It wasn't what she really liked, but then beggars couldn't be choosers, now could they?

She'd at least be independent and there was enough money hiding in the bottom of her trunk to purchase the few things she'd need for housekeeping, as well as keep her until she made a few dollars with the sewing machine. And the good-looking Sheriff Gabe Walker could just get over his snit when he found out that Garnet Dulan was the new dressmaker in the town of Frenchman's Ford, Nevada Territory. If he didn't like it, he could get on the next stage going east or west, and she'd apply for his job. Nothing in the books said a woman had to have a voice like honey to be a sheriff, did it?

She laughed at that idea. It would be a long time before women were allowed into the law enforcement field. Only a couple of years before had a woman been permitted ad-mittance to a college where she could get a degree to be a licensed medical doctor. And that had taken some kind of doing. It would be a long time before women had the right to do what men took for granted. But by golly, they could sew and if Betsy was right in her predictions, Garnet should be able to at least support herself with that bit of knowl-edge.

Thank you, Aunt Lulu. Aunt Lulu had insisted Garnet

learn the fine hand stitching and also to run the sewing machine when it was invented and made available to the public. Garnet hated the work in the beginning even if she did have a natural eye for design and creation.

She was about to unbutton her dress when she heard the scrape of the Sheriff's boots on the wooden floor. They stopped outside her door and she waited for him to knock, but he didn't. Thank goodness for small favors, she thought, as she listened intently to him go on down the hall and softly shut the door to his room. *One more night in this house with the Widow Nash about to hogtie me and drag me off to a temperance meeting, and the good sheriff ready to hogtie me and toss me on the next stage leaving Frenchman's Ford is enough to fry my nerves.*

She slipped out of her dress, corset and underwear and pulled one of her own soft, worn nightrails over her head. Tomorrow the rest of her life would begin and she could hardly wait for it to start.

Chapter Seven

Gabe slathered butter on his biscuits at the breakfast table and eyed Garnet. She seemed subdued and ready to admit that she'd lost the war, giving Gabe more mixed feelings than he wanted to admit. He'd enjoyed the battles this past week, and had even conjured up a little admiration for the woman who had the courage to stand up to him. He'd hand her a certain amount of respect, yes ma'am. But on the other hand he'd be glad to have her out of Frenchman's Ford. Out of sight; out of mind. At least that's what he sincerely hoped. Every night he dreamed about her. Either lying there on the cold ground, dead. Or else sending electric sparks through his body with the faintest brush of her hand across his when they passed in the hallway.

Garnet chewed slowly and swallowed tiny bites. She wondered if she'd ever be able to gulp a glass of tea without coming up for air again. But when she thought of the alternative, small bites and chewing slowly didn't seem too big a price to pay. Gabe wasn't his usual caustic self this morning, but then he probably thought he'd won. She'd let him keep his fragile bubble of contentment a while longer. All day, if he didn't press her.

She heard the wagon stop outside the house just as she finished the last of her coffee. *Tomorrow I'll make real coffee in my own house,* she thought and bit her tongue to keep from grinning. *And it will be dark as black strap molasses and strong enough to straighten my hair.* She opened the door for Matthew, who didn't look a thing like she'd pictured him. She'd thought he'd be a small man with thinning hair and spectacles perched on his skinny nose. The man standing outside on the porch with his straw hat in his hands was more than six feet tall, had wide shoulders and the thickest crop of red hair she'd ever seen. His bibbed overalls were faded but pressed without a wrinkle in them. His chambray work shirt stretched over muscles and a blue bandanna was tied around his neck.

"I understand I'm to move a trunk for you," he said in a deep, resonant voice. "And pick up a sewing machine at the store."

"Yes, sir," Garnet said. "If you'll follow me, I've got everything packed and ready."

"So which way are you going?" Gabe asked from so close behind her she wondered if he'd heard all of what Matthew had said.

"What difference does it make as long as I'm out of your way?" Garnet said.

"You got a point there," Gabe said. "I've got to go to Ullin this morning on sheriff's business. I'll go over to the general store and give Dusty enough money to buy your ticket whichever way you want to go before I leave. I had full intentions of putting you on that stage coach myself, but I see that you've come to your senses and realize there is nothing for you in Frenchman's Ford. It's been nice knowing you, Garnet," he stuck out his hand.

A wide grin split her face as she shook with him. "Liar," she said.

"Have you ever used your feminine wiles in your whole life?" he asked, his hand fairly well on fire from her touch.

"Not on stupid liars like you," she said. "Have a wonderful trip to Ullin. Tell that little boy hello for me."

"You going that way?" he asked.

"Not if you are," she said. "Good-bye, Gabe."

"Good-bye, Garnet Dulan," he said, an emptiness filling his heart and anger working its way through the rest of his body. He didn't care one whit where Garnet Dulan went; north, east, south, west. As long as he didn't have to see her on the streets of Frenchman's Ford. Soon, the talk would die down and she'd be no more than a story people told their kids and grandkids.

"Matthew?" She motioned for him to follow her up the steps.

He picked up the trunk and threw it up on his shoulder like it was filled with chicken feathers or duck down instead of weighing so much that Gabe had wrestled with it bringing it up the stairs just a week ago. "You wasn't real honest with him, you know," Matthew said, a smile twitching at the corners of his mouth. "Not that you was dishonest, but I think that might be classified as a sin of omission."

"Probably," she said. "But he's got business in Ullin. He don't have time to stand around here and fight with me all day. And I promise to do ten extra minutes on my knees praying for forgiveness for my sin of omission if you'll go real slow when you put that trunk in your wagon. Let's let the good sheriff leave town without a worry on his mind."

"You and Betsy going to make fine neighbors, and we're right glad to have a piano player in our church," Matthew said. "I reckon I could take my time loading up this trunk so the good sheriff has done what he needs to do over at the general store. It might keep his mind easy if we even watch him ride on out of town toward Ullin before we go in there and buy that machine. Just so there wouldn't be a disturbance today, you know. Not that I'm aiding and abetting a woman of a mind to go against what our good sheriff has insisted upon having."

"Why, Reverend . . ." she stopped. Betsy had never mentioned her last name and Garnet was at a lose for words.

"Not Reverend. The Good Book says that preachers should be leaders of the flock. That makes us shepherds, not Reverend or Pastor or even Brother. Sounds kind of pompous to me. So I'm just plain old Matthew Smith."

"Smith?" Her eyes widened. The man looked like a Viking and his name was Smith?

"Daddy was a plain old hard working Englishman. Momma was from Scotland. I got Daddy's size and Momma's red hair and temper. I'm afraid my daughter, Charity, got my red hair and more of my temper than a little girl is supposed to have. Be nice if she outgrows it and is more like her Momma when she's a grown woman. My Betsy is the sweetest woman on the whole earth. Some days I nearly get calluses on my knees from giving thanks to the Lord for giving Betsy to me and from praying that the Lord would teach me to curb that temper," he grinned.

Garnet was going to like the Smith family, she decided right then and there. And she was going to enjoy playing the piano in their church. Yes, sir, Garnet had found her place in the sun. It might not be the promised land, like her sisters had found, but hey, four out of five finding their own portion of the promised land was pretty good odds. If one of them had to be just happy instead of ecstatic and in love, then she'd be content with that lot.

"I think he's on his way now," Matthew's head bobbled just slightly at Gabe, who was riding a big, chestnut colored horse out of town. He didn't look back and Garnet was slightly disappointed.

"I'll walk down to the general store and have my purchases made before you get the wagon turned around and parked outside it. You got any idea what might be in the cabin?" She asked.

"Betsy left a feather mattress on the bed. It was pretty rustic when we got there but she made a few woman's changes to it. She took all her pots and pans and dishes though, so you might need a few of those kind of things," he said. "I figured she would have give you a list a mile long about what you needed."

"No, just a verbal one, and I'm so excited I've forgotten," Garnet said, watching Gabe until he rounded the corner at the end of town and disappeared. Talk about lightning and thunder in those blue eyes when he rode back into town and found she was putting down roots in a cabin right behind the church. Whew! She didn't especially look forward to weathering that storm, but faith and saints, she could do it. She'd walked across nigh on to half of America and she wouldn't be kicked out of a town. If she left, it would be of her own accord and when she was ready.

"Well, you'll be less than a quarter of a mile from the general store, so just get the basic things this morning, and make your own list. I'll be right glad to pick up whatever you need that you can't carry anytime you want me to," Matthew said.

"Thanks Matthew Smith," she said, a lightness in her step as she crossed the street to the other side and turned in the direction of the general store.

"So which way is it to be? Just tell Matthew to bring that trunk in and set it on the porch beside the door. The stage coach driver will load it for you from there," Dusty stood beside the door when she opened it. "Course now if you've a mind to stay in Frenchman's Ford, and want to take me up on that proposal?"

"No thank you on the proposal," she whispered. She wondered if she'd ever have a voice again; ever be able to scream or sing. Somehow she doubted it. "But I've a mind to purchase a few things today, Dusty. I want that sewing machine in the window. And that cast iron frying pan right there, two of those bread pans, that bean pot and a set of plain white sheets. Two sets of sheets, that is. This wool blanket and . . . are you making a list?"

He stood there dumbfounded, his beady little eyes barely slits behind his wire rimmed eye glasses. "The stage hands ain't going to carry all that stuff for you. Besides you can buy those things wherever you are going."

"I'm not going. I'm staying right here. I'm going to live in the cabin Zebediah built when he first came to town and

I'm the new seamstress and dress designer for Frenchman's Ford. So if you'll get your slate and make a list of what I want today, then we'll discuss what I want ordered in the way of lace and fabric so I can work," she said, the last few words really taxing her voice.

"Yes, ma'am, but Gabe Walker is going to go up in flames when he hears this," Dusty said.

"I hope so, and I'll shoot anyone who tries to put the flames out," Garnet said and began to point at the things she wanted. By the time Matthew opened the door, Dusty had most of it in a wooden crate and ready for him to load.

"Now, I see four bolts of satin and several hanks of black lace. Put all of that on hold for me and order more," she said.

"You crazy?" Dusty said. "Women in Frenchman's Ford ain't going to be buying fancy dresses like that. They want calico and gingham. Maybe some chambray for work day dresses."

"Order more of that, too," she smiled. "But don't forget the satin and lace. That's important."

"Okay, but Gabe is going to have a fit," Dusty shook his head. Garnet Dulan was sure enough going to have to come down off that pedestal she'd put herself up or else Gabe Walker was going to knock her off it. Lord, but he was going to be fit to be tied when he got home. And Dusty would probably be the one to have to tell him the news when he come in to see which way she went and how much money he had left from the bills he'd left to pay her fare.

"Gabe likes to have fits," Garnet said as she followed Matthew out the door.

The cabin was bigger than she'd imagined even if it was only one big room. A wide front porch set in a border of gold and orange marigolds and sported a swing on one end. The hewn logs fit together very well and the chinking looked good and solid. Garnet felt like hopping out of the wagon and dancing right there. A house of her very own.

She'd never had that before and it looked like a mansion sitting there in the middle of a sandy yard, just barely off the dusty road.

"It ain't much," Matthew said, grabbing up the trunk first and taking it inside. "Follow me, Garnet. This is your new home long as you play the piano at the church on Sundays. Zebediah is a strange little man, but a religious one. Wealthy as Midas and tight with it, except when it comes to the church. He adored his wife and she was a fine church-going woman. Guess that's where he gets it. Now where would you want me to put the trunk?"

Garnet stood in the middle of the large room in amazement. A small window with real glass was positioned in each side so she could see in every direction. Light filtered in through starched curtains made from feed sacks and tied back with bits of colorful ribbons. An oversized bed fashioned of logs with the bark left on them filled one corner, a cook stove and table with two benches and two chairs another side. An enormous stone fireplace set on one end with a rocking chair in front of it.

"The chair was Zebediah's wife's chair. She liked that fireplace so he left it there in memory of her. Said when you leave to please not take it with you," Matthew said.

"Put the sewing machine right there," she said, choosing a place not far from the table where she'd be cutting and designing dresses.

"Okay, then the rest of it can just set on the table?" he asked.

"That will be fine," Garnet said, the urge to hug herself and do a jig almost more than she could bear.

"Oh, and one more thing," Matthew said when he'd unloaded the last crate. "Charity sent this along. I told her you might not want it, and if that's the case then just bring it on back to our place. We just live back that road a ways. Close to the river so Betsy can have lots of water for her garden and flowers. She said she'll bring over some turnips and potatoes and other vegetables this afternoon, by the way. She had to visit a sick lady this morning out close to the mines. Woman just had a new baby and isn't getting back on her feet as fast as she did with the other six."

"Thank you," Garnet said. "What is it?" She eyed the wooden box with holes in the top.

"You just open it up and see. But wait until I'm gone. That way you'll have to keep it a day at least and Charity's feelings won't be hurt too bad. You can make up a story if you don't want it. Try to make it a good one so she won't throw a fit. She really did inherit my temper," he chuckled and backed out of the door.

Garnet scarcely waited until he was in the wagon before she lifted the top and stared down into the box at a little raven colored kitten with eyes the color of a summer sky. She picked it up, held it close to her heart and it immediately began to purr. As it snuggled down for more petting, tears filled Garnet's eyes. She had a home and a companion all in one fell swoop. Frenchman's Ford was going to be her home . . . whether Gabe Walker liked it or not.

"Thunder," she said. "I don't know if you are a boy or a girl cat, but your name is Thunder. You remind me of someone else with eyes just like yours and a black mood all the time."

The cat continued to purr and behold, if Garnet didn't feel her own heart doing the same thing.

By the time she had her bed made up proper and the few things she'd purchased put away, Betsy knocked at her door. She came in just long enough to give Garnet a hug and show her a trap door under the rug beside the fireplace that led down into a small root cellar. Together they unloaded a bushel of potatoes, turnips and a half bushel each of beets and carrots. Betsy also brought two crates with snap beans, corn and peas she'd canned through the summer months.

"Oh, my," Garnet fought back tears.

"Oh, don't you dare start weeping," Betsy said. "I been admiring all that steel in you these past days so don't you even think about shedding tears. You suck it up and be strong like us women in Frenchman's Ford want you to be. We don't want to follow after someone like Stella Nash with all her radical ideas, but we would like to make you feel right at home here because we need a woman with some backbone to help us out at times.'"Yes, ma'am," Garnet grinned, not knowing just what she could ever do to repay all the kindness she'd been shown.

"Oh, and the other women of the church will probably be stopping by for a few minutes. I understand Ruby Ann is bringing over some jars of canned tomatoes and the others, well, just be a gracious receiver today, Garnet," Betsy said. "Now I've got to run. Charity is reading to the boys but I've got their lessons to do. I just wish you had a voice so you could teach. Maybe though, when you get settled in you could teach her to play the piano. Momma tried to teach me when I was a little girl, but I just didn't have the ear for it. I can do a passable job on Sunday morning hymns but that's the extent of my musical abilities."

"I'd be glad to," Garnet said. "And tell her thanks for the kitten. I named it Thunder."

"Strange name for a cat but I guess you got your reasons. Charity picked it out of the litter for you because it was the only one with blue eyes. She said they wasn't as pretty as yours but they were blue," Betsy said as she hustled out the kitchen door and into the buggy.

Garnet waved from the back porch, holding Thunder close to her chest. She'd have to put some sand in a box and bring it in the house because Thunder was going to be an indoor cat. Betsy had turned the kitten upside down and declared that it was a girl cat, so her main job was to purr for Garnet and catch any stray mice brave enough to sneak into the cabin. For that she could have a nice warm bed beside the fire place, a clean box of sand every day, and all she could eat, plus Garnet's heart.

She'd barely made it back inside the house when there was a knock on the front door. Expecting to see someone named Ruby Ann, she put Thunder on the floor so she could explore and opened the door to find Emmy standing there.

"I hope it's all right that I come here," the girl said nervously. "I wouldn't want to make no trouble for you. I mean with you playin' the piano in the church and all."

"Come right in," Garnet said. First the preacher's wife and now the barmaid. Well, it couldn't be said that Garnet Dulan was a snob, now could it? "What I do in my home is my business."

"Well, I come for that yellow dress you promised me. I brought money," she said, coins jingling together in the velvet reticule she carried on her wrist. "And the other girls, they want to know where they can buy one kinda like it."

"Right here," Garnet whispered. "I'm going to make dresses like this one," she opened the trunk and brought it out for Emmy. "Tell the girls to come when they have time so I can measure them and I'll make fancy dresses for whoever wants to pay me to do it."

"Oh, wow," Emmy's eyes glistened as she fingered the yellow satin. "I can't believe this is mine. It's the prettiest thing I've ever seen. How much money do you want for it?"

Garnet gave her a price and Emmy's eyes flooded with tears. "That ain't enough for something this fine but I thank you for givin' it to me for that much. Now I'll have enough money to get another one made up. Can you measure me right now? I want another one so's I can keep them clean. How does a body wash this kind of thing? You know, it'll get dirty every night."

"Yes, I can measure you. Rub the soap into cold water until you make the water soapy then gently wash the dress in that water. Rinse it in clear water three times, and if you've got a little rosewater or lavender water, you could use that for the last rinse. Hang it to dry but don't wring it out. The dripping water will pull some of the wrinkles out. Iron it with a cloth between it and the iron." Garnet kept her voice at a very low whisper to keep from taxing it, but Emmy didn't miss a single word.

"Ain't got no rosewater," Emmy said.

"Well, there's some roses out there on my back porch," Garnet said. "I can make you some this week, and we'll have another dress for you by then. Change them out so they'll last longer. This one night, the new one another."

"I want one for every night of the week," Emmy said.

"What color?" Garnet measured the girl, amazed that she was indeed the same size as Garnet.

"You decide," Emmy said. "You fix them up like you see they'd look fine on me. I like this yellow just fine."

"I see you in lots of yellow," Garnet said. "From light yellow to the deepest gold."

"Then yellow is my color. The other girls can pick a different one. I'll be the new yellow rose of Texas in Nevada territory," Emmy giggled. "Now tell me what it is you do to your hair to make it shine like that."

Garnet reached out and touched the oily mess of straight deep chestnut hair. "Wash it every day. First thing when you wake up in the morning, wash your hair. We'll do it right now. Then I'm going to show you how to curl it. Once a week, put a half a cup of vinegar in the rinsing water, to cut the oil."

"Every day?" Emmy's brown eyes popped open so wide.

"It won't kill you and the men will love it," Garnet said.

"Then let's get after it," Emmy said, throwing her shawl over the back of a chair and removing the pins, holding it back in a slick bun at the nape of her neck.

Garnet washed it twice with pure lye soap and then rinsed it several times. The last time she rinsed it she used the vinegar treatment and then dried it on her own bathing towel she'd just bought that morning. She'd never seen such dirty water from a mere hair washing, and was glad she hadn't found lice hiding in the greasy mess. When Emmy's hair was barely damp she drug out an old petticoat from her trunk, took her scissors and cut it into strips an inch wide and eight inches long.

"Oh, my, don't you be tearin' up your things," Emmy fussed.

"Shhh," Garnet put her finger on her mouth and shook her head. She'd already talked more than she should that day but she wasn't going to let Emmy wear her yellow satin without pretty hair to go with it. Using her comb, she separated the hair into sections and wrapped it around the rags she'd made from the petticoat. She handed Emmy the small hand mirror she carried in her trunk and made her watch the procedure so she could train the other girls to do the same thing.

Emmy was mesmerized by the whole procedure.

"Take a bath every night or every morning," Garnet said. "Menfolks like to see clean women. Wash your hair, roll it on the rags. Don't brush it when you take it down. Just run your fingers through the curls to separate them. Put on your headpiece to hold the curls back and you'll be ready to rake in the money."

"Oh, Miss Garnet I owe you so much. We all will. I'll send Rosy over tomorrow," Emmy said. "She's just green with envy that I'm getting this dress."

"Pinks," Garnet said.

"And Goldie?" Emmy asked.

"Greens," Garnet answered, not telling Emmy that she'd envisioned the girls in their finery from the first night. Except then she'd seen Emmy in green and Goldie in the yellows. She changed her mind when she realized how pale Goldie would look in the yellow and how rich her blonde hair would appear in emerald green.

"And Pansy in purple," Emmy said.

Garnet gave her a bright smile.

"I can't very well walk down the street with my hair lookin' like this," Emmy said. "I look horrible."

Garnet picked up Emmy's shawl and used it to cover her head, letting the bottom flow down her back.

"Thank you for everything," Emmy said. "But most of all thank you for letting me come right in your home and making me welcome. I'll tell the girls to come around tomorrow to be measured. And there'll be a hair washin' and curlin' when I get back to the Silver Dollar today."

Garnet waved from the front porch, sat down on the swing and planned out what kind of dress she would start later that day for Emmy. She'd have to make a trip to the general store but there had been a bolt of satin there a deep shade of gold that would look marvelous on the girl. No sooner had Emmy rounded the corner where the church sat, when another buggy pulled by a big white horse came toward the cabin, stopping when it reached the yard.

"I'm Ruby Ann. I brung you some things," a chubby woman jumped down from the seat. "Was that one of the bar girls leavin' here?"

"Yes, it was," Garnet said.

"Well, that'd be your business. I hear you're goin' to be sewing?" Ruby Ann picked up a box and carried it to the porch and went back for another one.

"Yes, I am," Garnet said.

"That's good. We'd be needin' a seamstress in this town. I'll put in an order for a half a dozen shirt waists. Can't buy a blessed thing to fit a woman made up like I am. I can get the skirts from the mail order catalog, but the tops, now that is a different matter. You want to measure me right now while you got me here? I'll take them in calico, plaid, gingham and chambray," Ruby Ann said.

"I sure will, and thanks so much," Garnet said. "You got time for a cup of coffee?"

"I'll make time," Ruby Ann said, a wide smile cutting through a face full of freckles. "I lead the singin' at the church so you and me, we'll be workin' together. You goin' to sew up fancy dresses for them other women?"

"Yes, I am," Garnet opened the door and let Ruby go inside the cabin ahead of her.

"I reckon that's all right. Woman has got to do what a

woman has got to do when she ain't got a man to provide for her. Just don't be puttin' no fancy laces or frills on my shirts, honey. I got so much up on top that it don't need no frills to draw attention to it. Just make 'em plain with buttons down the front so I can get on them easy," she said.

And just like that Garnet had her work cut out for the next week. Whether Gabe Walker liked it or not. What amazed her even more than the fact that she already had so much to do, was that so many people already knew about it. Dusty must have spread the word as soon as she left the store.

Chapter Eight

A glorious sunset greeted Gabe Walker as he rode back into Frenchman's Ford that evening. Fall was doing a fine job of pushing the summer of 1860 into the history books. There was a nip in the air that signaled it wouldn't be long until the snows began. Gabe was sure the high places already had white caps. The meeting in Ullin had gone even better than he'd expected. He'd had a sit-down meeting with other area sheriffs who were concerned about the recent Paiute Indian uprising. The government had moved the tribe north into Gabe's territory and guaranteed that by the next year they'd have a fort built south of Frenchman's Ford and have it manned with enough soldiers to take care of things. The Paiute were still angry about being uprooted from their native ground and still in a rage about two Indian girls who'd been kidnapped and abused by white men. The white settlers were still in an uproar about the retaliation the tribe had dealt out to the white men who'd kept the girls in captivity. But in a year, maybe all their feathers would be soothed and peace would reign again. At least the government was building a fort and sending protection.

Yes, it had gone well and now he was back home. Back home where Garnet wasn't. Even though she haunted his dreams every night, he was glad she wouldn't be there.

He'd made a big mistake when he didn't believe her story or even check it out before he threw her in jail, and that's why she kept appearing in his dreams. In a few weeks though, that would cease and she'd just be the pretty lady with red hair who played the piano in the Silver Dollar for one night.

He left his horse at the livery with instructions that he be given an extra portion of feed that night. He walked down the street past the church. No services tonight so it was dark inside. A picture of Garnet moving away from him and going inside that building surfaced. He tried to shake off the memory. He literally shook his shoulders and head to get rid of the image branded on his mind. He peeked in the window at the jail and saw Deputy Les Watkins leaning back in the chair with his feet propped on the desk. His hands were laced behind his head and his eyes were shut. Yes, sir, Gabe had surely left Frenchman's Ford in capable hands. He slung open the door and Les tried to jump but ended up pushing himself backwards with his feet. The chair and Deputy Les both landed back down and facing the ceiling.

"See you got everything under control," Gabe said.

"I sure do," Les dusted the seat of his pants off with a brush of his palms. "Been quiet as a church mouse ever since you left. Not a murder one. No bank robberies. Not one blame thing for me to haul anyone in here for. Guess that'll all change with the weekend though. I been keepin' watch 'til about midnight and then goin' on home to get some sleep. But I been back on the job by seven ever morning."

"That's right good news, Les. I reckon since I'm back in town and we don't have a prisoner to watch, you can go on home and get you some real sleep tonight. I'll take care of things until midnight or thereabouts," Gabe said. "Anything else unusual happening in town?"

"Well," Les chewed the inside of his lip. He sure hated to be the one to tell Gabe that Garnet Dulan had set up house right behind the church in that cabin Zebediah built. "No, can't say there has been anything unusual. Just a quiet town while you been gone."

"That's good," Gabe said. "Now get on outta here before I change my mind and make you sleep in that chair until midnight."

"I'll do it," Les said, eager to be gone before Gabe found out about Garnet. There'd be fireworks for sure when he realized she'd just plain gone against what Gabe had told her to do. But dang it all, she'd sure enough played a pretty piano in church on Sunday morning.

Gabe double checked everything in the jail before he strolled on down the sidewalk toward the Silver Dollar. Dusty was just locking up the store for the day as he passed. Gabe rolled his blue eyes toward the stars in the dark skies. Dusty always wanted to stop and visit forever at the close of the day. Being a bachelor and living alone in a house just south of the church, he got lonely of an evening. Not being a drinking man, he wasn't inclined to spend any time in either of the two saloons, so Gabe had learned early on to avoid the man when he was closing shop.

"Evenin' Gabe," Dusty said, more than a little nervous. From the peaceful look on Gabe's face, no one had told him yet, and Dusty would sell his stock and relocate to the middle of Hades before he was the bearer of bad news. He'd read in the old times how they shot the messenger, and with Gabe's temper, it wouldn't be a surprise if the good sheriff did draw his pistol out, shoot first and ask questions later. No, sir, Dusty might not be the brightest star in the sky, but he wasn't downright stupid.

"Evenin' Dusty," Gabe said.

"Well, I'm goin' home and catch up on my newspaper readin'," Dusty said, walking away from Gabe so fast that it just plumb spooked the sheriff.

"Hey, Dusty," Gabe called out to the fast disappearing

black shadow headed down the sidewalk in a near run. "Did I leave you enough money for that stage ticket?"

"Oh, yes, come on by tomorrow and we'll talk about it," Dusty kept walking, even faster.

"Wonder what's come over him?" Gabe said aloud. His boots made a scraping sound on the wooden sidewalk as he passed the Spur. He opened the door and peeked in briefly, but the saloon was quiet. Almost too quiet. Two old-timers were bellied up to the bar, talking so softly Gabe couldn't even hear what they were saying. The barkeep waved but didn't motion him inside so he shut the door and crossed the street.

A tingle crept up his spine. Something wasn't right. He could feel it in his bones. Frenchman's Ford had never been like this. Not even on a weeknight. The silver miners were always coming in to spend their money and raise the dickens. Gabe noticed the owner of the lumber yard, Ruby Ann's husband, Cletus, was sitting at his desk just behind the glass window. Gabe tapped on the window and the man looked like he'd seen a ghost when he looked up. He quickly pointed toward his books and bent his head back over them without inviting Gabe inside.

The itch on Gabe's neck intensified. Cletus liked to talk even more than Dusty. Even more than the barkeep at the Spur. Yes, something was definitely wrong in his town. And he knew just where to go to get his answers. Jonah kept a heavy finger on the pulse of the town and he'd know exactly what was happening. Did the whole town have a meeting while he was gone and fire him, or had Frenchman's Ford been taken over by a bunch of gun slinging bandits?

He stepped inside the Silver Dollar and knew immediately what the problem was no one wanted to discuss with him. There it stood next to the bar talking to Jonah. He'd never forget that yellow dress trimmed in black lace. So Garnet had talked Jonah into putting her back to work, and she hadn't left town at all. Jonah had been his best friend for as long as Gabe could remember, but Jonah betrayed that friendship and a rage mounted inside Gabe like a bull who'd just seen the red cape of a bull fighter.

In five easy steps he was across the saloon and had the woman by the arm, surprised that the burning sensation wasn't there when he touched her. He swung her around, expecting to look down into those strange colored eyes with lightning flashing in them. She pulled away from him so fast that he blinked and when he opened his eyes it was Emmy he was staring at. Emmy, wearing Garnet's yellow dress. Emmy with her chestnut hair so shiny and curly that in the dim light she'd looked like Garnet from behind.

"Well, Gabe Walker, I see you are back in town but that don't give you no cause to be getting rough with me," Emmy said with a toss of her hair, making the feathers fly out and float down gracefully back to her shoulders.

"Where'd you get that dress?" he asked roughly.

"I bought it from Garnet Dulan. I think it's a shame you and Jonah are so pig-headed you wouldn't give her a job here in the saloon," Emmy said. "Now I've got work to do, if you think you can keep your hands off me."

She picked up four mugs of beer, two in each hand and left him standing there with his mouth open. One thing for sure, she wasn't telling him that Garnet hadn't left Frenchman's Ford. No way. She valued the job she had and the dress she was wearing too much for that kind of thing. Gabe might go out there to that cabin, lock Garnet in the jail and really sell her off to the Indians like he'd threatened to do. And Emmy was going to have more pretty dresses before anything like that happened. Since she brought the dress home, she'd been the favored one. The other barmaids had been fair sports about it since Garnet had guaranteed they'd have costumes by the end of next week, though. One a week as long as they wanted to pay for them. Their sewing came first above even the proper ladies in the town, she'd said, since they were the ones who'd given her the idea for her new job.

"Gabe?" Jonah set a tall glass of tea in front of him. "Meeting go well?"

"Wonderful. They've already signed the treaty and the uprisings should be over for a while. That is if we can keep the white men from grabbing a couple of Indian girls and hurting them again. There's some renegade factions out there but for the most part Chief Winnemucca is willing to make peace," Gabe said.

"Might last a month. Could last 'til spring," Jonah said.

"Something's different," Gabe said.

"Yeah, sure is. Look at them girls. All clean with their hair curled up. You should see them in the mornings, primping and then they look like a bunch of little school girls with their hair tied up in rags all day long. But it's making a difference, Gabe. I swear it is. Men folks come in here just to look at Emmy in that yellow dress. They call her the yellow rose of Texas. She just laughs and tells them she's the yellow rose of Nevada Territory," Jonah said. Gabriel Walker could pull out his toenails with pliers before he'd tell him that Garnet Dulan was the cause of his barmaids looking so good and on the edge of looking even better.

"So what made the difference?" Gabe said.

"They got it in their heads that if they were dolled up, there'd be more men in here and I'd give them a raise. They're right. I make more money, I'll see to it they get a fair share of it." Jonah wiped down the bar without looking at Gabe.

"Well, that's a fact. The Spur looks like a morgue. Two old men in there discussing the stars. Town is so quiet it's plump spooky. If I didn't know better I'd swear I wasn't walkin' down the streets of Frenchman's Ford where there's two or more killings a week," Gabe said.

"Don't worry. It'll fire up right quick later in the week.

I got a few miners in tonight for the brew, but the weekend will bring them in in droves. 'Specially when these boys go back and tell the others about the yellow rose," Jonah said.

"Anything else going on I should know about?" Gabe asked cautiously. Even Jonah avoided looking him in the eye.

Jonah shook his head and turned his back to fill four mugs for a tray Pansy had just set on the bar. "And a shot of your best whiskey," Pansy said.

"How are things going?" Gabe asked Pansy.

"Just fine. Never been better," she smiled brightly at him. Mercy, but he was going to be madder'n a wet hen after a fresh rain when he found out, but it wasn't going to be from Pansy's lips. Not in a million years. She fully well intended to have that lovely purple dress with lots of black lace next week, then she'd show Emmy just who the prettiest barmaid in the saloon was. Those silver miners were sure free with their money when they had something nice to look at. Who'd have ever thought giving their hair a good washing every morning and tying it up in rags could make such a difference? When they got their dresses, there'd be even more difference.

"Hair looks right nice. Who taught you to fix it like that?" Gabe asked.

"Emmy learned how and taught the rest of us. 'Scuse me Gabe. I got a bunch of thirsty men over there," Pansy picked up the tray and sidestepped around him.

"So everything run just fine without me?" Gabe asked Jonah.

"I suppose it did. We managed here at the Silver Dollar. You'd have to check with Les to see about anything else," Jonah said.

"Then I'm going back to the jail and do a little paper work before I turn in. Maybe I'm the one who's causing the trouble in Frenchman's Ford," Gabe tried to chuckle but it came out almighty flat.

"Could be you're the one who's cleaned it up so well you can go off for three or four days and nothing happens because no one wants to face your wrath if it does," Jonah said.

"You trying to tell me something?" Gabe asked, narrowing his eyes.

"I'm not telling you nothing," Jonah said.

"Then I'm going to the jail and at midnight I'm going to bed. You remember anything you want to tell me just send one of the girls and I'll come right on back down here," Gabe said. "Because there's something going on and I'll find out one way or the other, Jonah."

Not by my mouth you won't, Jonah thought as he nodded and went back to work.

At eleven o'clock, when he'd run everything in the world past his mind and tried to figure out what had happened to his town while he was gone, he finally closed the jail doors and went across the street, peeped inside the bank window just to make sure everything was in order and on down to the boarding house. He opened the never locked door and tiptoed up the stairs. Stella had told him when she rented him a room that she kept to early evenings so she could arise before daylight. She realized he often had to keep late hours but he would have to be quiet when he came and went after dark.

He poured water from the pitcher into the matching bowl with pink flowers on the side and washed up before he stretched his long frame out on the soft mattress. He laced his hands behind his head and listened to the night sounds—the dull sound of the last hour of the saloon down the street; crickets singing their final duets with the frogs and one lonesome coyote telling the moon what he thought of the condition of his life. Everything was in order, after all. Nothing was wrong in his town. Nothing could be wrong. He'd simply read the signs wrong. Not often did that happen to Gabriel Walker, but he made a mistake every once in a while. Tonight was one of them. He shut his eyes tightly and went right to sleep . . . only to dream of Garnet in the yellow dress, asking him if she was indecent enough to play the piano in his town now.

The next morning he shaved in his room with cold water to keep from going down to the kitchen and listening to Stella rant and rave about the evils of liquor. He opened the wardrobe and took out a clean shirt and trousers. When he'd dressed, he slipped his arms into one of his many black leather vests and pulled his boots on. His stomach growled and he found himself hoping that there would be other boarders at the table that morning. Someone to talk to, to share breakfast with. Someone to take his mind off Garnet.

Stella was at the stove, just dishing up a plate of scrambled eggs with a side order of bacon. She was the only person in the kitchen and she looked like she was ready to deliver him a sermon guaranteed to scorch the hairs out of Lucifer's nose.

"Good morning, Stella," he said. "Hope I come in quiet enough last night."

"I heard you. But then I was still awake so I can't fuss at you for it. I was just so mad I could just spit tacks. Can you believe they'd actually let her play the piano at the church house when she's sewing for those evil women? Those that sell liquor to the men folks of this town. That's right, Gabe Walker, she's sewing dresses for them. Fancy dresses to take our men's minds away from their little children and faithful wives. And then she sits right up there in the church house building and plays the piano like she was a saint fallen straight out of Heaven itself. Ask me, I'd tell you the whole town of Frenchman's Ford is crazy as a cross-eyed Missouri mule. But did anyone ask me? No they didn't ask me one thing. Eat your eggs before they get cold. Ain't nothing in this world worse than greasy cold eggs," she rambled on and on.

That prickly itch crawled from his neck over the top of

his head. He scratched at it with every finger on his right hand but it didn't go away. "I can't see Matthew letting Betsy sew for them women. And last I heard she didn't play the piano worth listening to. They got a new woman in town while I was gone?"

"No they did not!" Stella propped her hands on her hips and glared at him. "You just up and trusted her to do what you said and didn't stay around to see it through. Some sheriff you are, Gabe Walker. You think if you told the Silver Dollar to shut its doors because your landlady said so, it would shut its doors? No, it would not. You got rocks for brains some days, Sheriff. That's a fact and you can write it down on a big old slab of stone because it's the gospel according to Stella Nash."

"You want to tell me exactly what you are talking about?" Gabe felt the muscles in his stomach tighten up and his jaws began to ache from clenching them.

"Why of course, I'll tell you what I'm talking about," Stella said. "You said for her to leave but you just rode out of town and figured she was going to do your bidding. Well, she didn't, Gabe Walker. She and that preacher's wife, the one who won't even join my temperance group and try to put an end to the vile evil of liquor, they got their heads together and she's put in a seamstress shop back behind the church house in that cabin Zebediah built when he come to town. Let her have it free of charge if she'll play the piano at the church when we gather. And the rest of the God fearin' women in town is suddenly blind as cactus to the sewing she's doin' for the saloon girls. If she'll sew for them, they say it's none of their business who else she sews for. Ruby Ann done told me that much when she come to church in a new calico shirtwaist. Well, I'm tellin' you one thing, she ain't sewing for me," Stella said, ice hanging on every word.

"You are telling me Garnet Dulan is still in town?" Gabe gritted through his teeth.

"Like I said you got rocks for brains. I been tellin' you

that since you walked in here this mornin', man. Didn't your Les or your good friend Jonah tell you last night when you come into town? Well, like I said, the whole town has done gone dumb and deaf, too," Stella said.

Gabe threw down the napkin he'd tucked into his shirt collar and pushed his chair away from the kitchen table so fast that the chair tumbled backwards with a loud thud. He stormed out the front door and across the street. He wouldn't be thwarted and made a fool of—not in his town. Garnet might have pulled the wool over the good citizens of Frenchman's Ford for a few days, but the gig was up. She was leaving town. And Dusty, Jonah and Cletus, as well as the barkeep at the Spur had sure better walk on egg shells for a month around him, or they'd be following in her footsteps.

Chapter Nine

Garnet had run a gathering seam across the top of ten yards of black lace and was doing the tedious job of pulling the seam a few inches at a time, creating the ruffle she intended to use around the neckline of Pansy's new fancy dress. The heavy knock on the door caused her to drop the lace but at least she didn't break the running thread. Figuring it was Pansy coming to check on the progress, she yelled for the visitor to come in.

The door swung open and Thunder took off in a frantic scamper. She went after the cat without even looking up to see who was coming inside her humble little cabin and ran straight into Gabe's broad chest, bounced back two steps and looked up into those blue eyes filled with more than thunder this time. So the good sheriff had made it back to Frenchman's Ford and realized she hadn't left.

"If you'll get out of my way, I've got to catch my cat," she said.

"Forget the cat," he growled.

She pushed past him, ignoring the heat radiating from a red hot anger and was on the porch calling for her cat before he could turn around.

"Garnet Dulan, I demand that you listen to me," he said.

"Keep your demands to yourself. I'll talk to you after I

catch my kitten. You want to talk sooner than that, I suggest you start helping me," she bowed up to him, her nose barely an inch from his.

For just a fraction of a second, he thought about kissing her. Those full lips looked so inviting and warm. All that beautiful red hair pulled back in a ribbon and cascading down her back; he had the craziest notion that he'd like to sink his fingers into it and draw her even closer.

Garnet watched as tenderness replaced thunder for just a moment and wanted to lean closer and see what had made the difference. But the soft edges were replaced with jagged ice in a single blink. His heavy eyebrows drew down and his jaw muscles worked in so much rage, she feared that he might actually pick her up bodily and really sell her to some strange named Indian tribe.

"You'll talk to me now," he demanded and held the door open for her to come back inside with him.

"I said I'll talk when I catch Thunder," she said. "You can wait inside. Don't sit in the rocker. I've got parts of a dress layin' all over it."

The growling of a stray dog took her attention from Gabe and back to the cat who'd crawled under the porch. The dog stuck his head under the end of the wooden porch and barked; the cat retaliated by scratching the dog's nose. Garnet kicked the dog's hind legs about the same time and it came out howling for mercy. It took off down the road and was still running like a gazelle when it rounded the corner at the church and headed down the main street of town.

Garnet stooped low and reached her hand back under the porch but only got a scratch for her efforts. She jerked her hand back and tried sweettalking the cat but nothing seemed to convince the little black ball of fur that it was safer in her arms than under the porch.

"Oh for Pete's sake," Gabe threw up his hands in surrender. He stretched his frame out on the porch, belly down and head leaning over the end of the porch. The kitten was content to tease Garnet and didn't see Gabe. With a swift thrust of his arm, he had it by the scruff of the neck.

"Don't you hurt her," Garnet said. "Give her to me. You've probably scared the life from her little body."

"Not me. I can't scare the life from anyone or anything," he muttered under his breath.

"Stop your fuming," Garnet said, taking the kitten inside and cooing over it like it was a baby. "She hasn't learned that she's an inside cat just yet. We're working on educating her to be a nice kitty cat."

Gabe followed Garnet, carefully closing the door behind him. Every available place except the chair she'd pulled up in front of that brand new sewing machine was covered with some part of her projects. Pieces of purple satin draped all over the big rocking chair. The bed was covered in yellow satin with a pattern made from newspaper held down by forks, spoons and knives.

"As you can see I'm busy so what is it that you need?" Garnet asked.

"I told you to leave town," he said.

"And I told you I wasn't going to," she whispered. What she'd give to be able to scream and yell at the top of her lungs couldn't be measured in silver and gold. She'd love to open the door, get right in his face and paint him some explicit directions on just how he could take the trip to hell on a rusty poker and what he could do when he got there.

"I can't make you go. Not now," he said. "But I don't have to like it. You've . . ."

"I've what Sheriff Walker? Found a house to live in? Have two jobs? Am supporting myself? I'm not asking you for one thing. Because of you I'll probably always talk in a whisper, but I'm making my own way. You can get out of my house and don't darken my door again. You are not welcome here," she said, the stiffness of her back betraying just how upset she was.

Gabe didn't know of a single house or business in

Frenchman's Bend where he wasn't welcome. The idea that he couldn't go anywhere with a warm welcome awaiting him slashed through him like a double edged sword. He stood there in the middle of the single room—speechless.

"Hey, anybody home?" The back door opened and Charity rushed in, all in a hurry like a little girl who ran everywhere and never wasted time walking.

"Come in Charity," Garnet said.

"Oh, Gabe, you done got home," Charity said. "Well, I'm glad you didn't get scalped by those Indians. They'll do that you know. Just slice your head open right here," she swiped her forefinger across the top of her forehead. "And then they grab hold of that skin and just tear it off your head. Tommy said he'd seen a man one time that didn't die when they scalped him and it was just awful looking. Anyway, I'm glad they didn't tear all your hair out. You woulda looked funny with a bald head. Oh, Garnet, I come to tell you that Momma is makin' soup today and she's bringing you a jar for your supper so you ain't to cook nothing. She said she'll bring cornbread to go with it. That way you don't have to stop your sewing. Oh, my is this Pansy's new fancy dress? You know I might grow up to be a barmaid if I can wear pretty shiny dresses like this." She ran to the rocking chair and wiped her hands on her skirt tail before she touched the fabric.

"Your Pa would have your hide for talkin' like that young lady," Gabe said, finally finding his own voice.

"He might. I'm either going to be a bar lady or else I'm joinin' up with Stella's temperance group. You know I heard them say at their meeting last night that they're going to take clubs and work over the saloons. On Saturday night, they're going to beat the mirrors above the bars to smithereens. What's a smithereen anyway?" Charity asked.

Garnet's racing heart settled down as she listened to Charity's ramblings. A smile twitched at the corners of her mouth as she stood back and let all that information and questions bounce off Gabe. Maybe by the time he'd explained everything to Charity, his mood would be better. It didn't matter, though, if he grew big old white wings and spoke with the tongues of sages when he answered the child, when he walked off her porch, she didn't ever want to see him again.

"What were you doing going to one of those meetings?" Gabe asked.

"I didn't go to the meeting, silly old man. They don't let girls join until they get married and have a bunch of kids. That's so they'll have a husband, you know. Someone to worry about drinking liquor with those pretty barmaids. And kids to make the husbands feel all guilty cause they drank up the money the wife was going to buy winter shoes for the kids with. That's why little girls can't join. They don't understand none of that stuff."

"If you weren't at that meeting then how'd you know what they said?" Gabe asked.

"Ruby Ann told Momma she was going to the temperance meeting at Stella's house. It was a hot night and I knew they'd leave the window open, so I just sneaked over there and sat down under the window. Stella sure does get all riled up, don't she? Well, I gotta go. Momma said I couldn't stay and visit because I got to read to the boys for a whole hour this afternoon. Boy, do I hate to read to them. They don't listen too good," Charity said. "Bye now. Are you goin' to kiss him good-bye, Garnet?"

"I am not!" Garnet blushed five shades of scarlet.

"Well," Charity sighed and laid the back of her hand on her forehead. "I sure wish you was so I could watch. I got to learn how to do that so I can catch a husband. You know I can't be a temperance woman without one. Guess I'll just have to watch Momma and Daddy closer and see if I can catch them kissin'."

In a flurry even more furious than the one she'd arrived in, she ran out the back door and back down the road. Garnet and Gabe avoided each other's eyes. Garnet looked at the strip of lace she'd been gathering. Suddenly, Gabe was interested in whatever he could see outside the window facing the church.

"Guess I'd better be on duty Saturday night if the temperance movement is up to shenanigans," he finally said, more to himself than to Garnet.

"It'll take radicals like Stella to cut a path for women folks," Garnet said. "Things don't get changed by folks just saying words. There has to be action."

"You going to join them in bashing the saloons on Saturday night?" He turned abruptly, their glares fighting across the room with each other.

"No, I am not!" Garnet hissed. "But that don't mean I can't see what she's trying to do. It's just that she's going about it all wrong."

"And how would you go about it?" Gabe asked.

"I'm not having a discussion with you. I'm not talking to you about anything. You'll keep Rosy and Pansy and the other girls safe, won't you?" she asked, real fear rising in her chest for the girls she'd befriended.

"Afraid you'll lose your business and have to leave town?" he asked.

Garnet stuck her nose in the air, folded her arms over her chest, turned her back to him and began to tap her foot on the floor. Thunder let out a pitiful meow, jumped from the window sill and made a dive under the bed. Garnet immediately went to the window, expecting to see the same mangy mutt in her yard. Next week she'd beg Matthew to make her a sling shot and she'd gather a basket of rocks. She'd been a good shot with one when she was a kid and she bet she could still put the fear of a flung rock into a dog if she had the chance.

But there was no dog in sight. The kitten let out another wail from under the bed and Garnet started in that direction when suddenly the whole house began to tremble. In that half second before Garnet realized what was happening, she felt like she was back in the stagecoach coming from Arkansas to St. Joseph, Missouri. One of the other occupants said that it felt like they were riding a ship in a storm. Garnet had never had opportunity to go anywhere on a ship, but suddenly she knew what the man was talking about. Her little cabin swayed. Pots flew from the shelves where she had them neatly placed. The rocking chair fell over on its side. Thunder set up a rueful howl under the bed that made Garnet's skin crawl, it was so pathetic.

One minute she was weaving from one side to the other. The next she heard Gabe say something about an earthquake. By the third, she and Gabe were both tossed like two limp ragdolls on the bed. As quickly as it began, it ended. Only when it started, they were across the room from each other. When it finished, they were in each other's arms, lying across a length of satin on a feather bed. His arms were wrapped tightly around her and her face was buried in his broad chest.

"Is it over?" she whispered, wondering for the life of her where the anger had gone and why she felt so at home snuggled up to the sheriff in her bed.

"The worst," he mumbled, inhaling the clean smell of her hair. Was that rose scent? "Might have a tremor or two later in the day, but this is probably the worst for now. We're used to these little ones. Comes along every so often in these parts. Your first?"

She looked up at him and nodded.

"You'll get used to them after a couple of years," he said, then wanted to bite his tongue off. She wouldn't be here in two years. Not if he had his way about it. He wanted her gone last week. He sure didn't want her to stay in Frenchman's Ford permanently.

He leaned forward and she stretched her neck at the same time. Their lips met and the earthquake was a minor act of God compared to the explosion inside their hearts. Garnet fought with her own staggering emotions while Gabe's lips claimed hers. Her heart wanted the kiss to go on forever and ever. Her mind wanted to pull back and slap pure fire from his face for presuming that he had the right to kiss her.

Neither won.

He'd pulled away and was on his feet, his hat retrieved from the floor where he'd dropped it when the quake hit, and was at the front door by the time she could refocus her vision after she opened her eyes.

"I can't do nothing about you being in Frenchman's Ford, Garnet Dulan. Not now. But I don't have to like it. Good day to you. And that wasn't anything special. It was just a kiss because we were put in an awkward situation, being thrown together on the bed like that. Don't be thinkin' it means one thing," he said with his hand on the door knob.

"The only thing special about it is that it'll never happen again so it's one of a kind." She was on her feet, high color filling her cheeks and gingerly picking her way around her things strewn on the floor.

"Good-bye." He tipped his hat as he shut the door behind himself.

"Forever," she mouthed as she began to tidy up the mess the earthquake had caused. At least her two good plates and cups had been in the dishpan and weren't broken into smithereens, like Charity had said about the saloon mirrors.

Gabe touched his mouth as he walked back toward town to see if there had been damage at the jail or at the Silver Dollar. It was cool to the touch, not on fire like it felt when he'd pulled away from the kiss. He wasn't a young teenager. He'd kissed women before. Lots of them. Once upon a time he'd even been engaged to a lady. When Jonah came and told him that he was the biggest fool in all of Kentucky for letting the woman lead him around by the nose, he and Jonah had had a severe falling out. A few weeks later he'd found out his friend was right and he was wrong. That was the other time he'd had to apologize.

But that kiss he'd shared with Garnet was mind-boggling and passionate. The whole world had stood still for a moment there and he'd wanted to spend the rest of his life right there in that cabin with her. Now wasn't that a frightening idea. She'd have him torn into shreds within a day with her sharp tongue. He felt sorry for any man who tried to tame that red-haired piece of baggage. They'd have a lifetime job of nothing but pure misery.

Garnet's fingers were as light as butterflies' wings when she touched her lips to see if they were still warm from Gabe's kiss. She'd had fumbling kisses from a few men but nothing that compared to the feelings evoked when the room stopped shaking and she found herself wrapped in his arms, nothing like the frantic emotions she'd experienced when she didn't want the kiss to end.

But end it did. Forever, just like she said when he declared it had just happened and wasn't anything serious. As if she'd declare that he'd have to marry her on the spot because he kissed her. Good grief, she wasn't a schoolgirl anymore. A grown woman didn't make men stand up at the altar and say "I do," because of one shared kiss. What confounded her was all those emotions she hadn't even known existed. Hadn't realized in all her years were lying dormant. Like a tulip bulb in the winter months. Just waiting for the spring rains and the warmth of the sun to bring it to life again.

Would there be a man out there who'd awaken those emotions again or was it just Gabe Walker? Now that was a scary thought. Surely it was just the high strung sensation of being alive when moments before the whole world had been shaking around her.

She continued to pick up the room and worry, examining her own feelings for the better part of an hour. When she sat back down at the sewing machine to gather the black lace into a ruffle for the dress she was working on, everything seemed the same. She was a seamstress even if she did like playing a fast piano better. She'd enjoyed the sweet sounds she'd produced from the old church piano on Sunday, though. She'd especially liked the people who were so nice to her. She'd fit in with everyone else in Frenchman's Ford and maybe someday a man would come along who made her feel giddy and see sparks like Gabe Walker did.

She laid the ruffle down after a few minutes. Nothing was the same. Her entire life had been turned around, upside down and backwards in the space of a three minute hurricane. She picked up Thunder who'd finally ventured out from under the bed and sat down in the rocking chair. She wouldn't hide behind a veil of denial. The man had affected her like she'd never been effected before.

But she could and would get over it. Like he said, it wasn't anything special. And he'd never be walking up on her porch or in her house again. She might see him on the street but that wasn't a big deal either. She'd kissed Dalhart Morris when she was sixteen, back behind the barn after a dance in Arkansas. She'd had to sit beside his mother the next morning in church and she'd lived through that, so she could live through seeing Gabe Walker on the streets of Frenchman's Ford.

After all she wasn't still sixteen. She was an grown woman and she'd been on her own for years. She'd walked across half the continent; she'd been hung and lived through it. She'd outwitted Gabe and stayed in Frenchman's Ford. She'd ignore him. That's what she'd have to do.

Sure, and at least fifty times a day you'll touch your lips to see if they are still warm and you'll remember, her conscience said bluntly.

"Hush," she whispered hoarsely, hugging the cat to her. "We don't need anyone do we, Thunder? Not anyone."

Garnet didn't believe one word of it and her heart continued to ache.

Thunder snuggled down and was content to be rocked.

Chapter Ten

Garnet pinned her red hair back at the nape of her neck, donned her dark blue Sunday dress and a new hat she'd designed that week. She'd seen it at the general store and immediately envisioned it decorated with bits of lace, a big satin ribbon wrapped around the crown and gathered into a bow in the back where she'd turned the brim up flat to allow room for her bun. She checked her reflection in the mirror and loved the way she'd taken that man's plain old straw hat and turned it into a nice fall Sunday hat. Maybe if she kept everyone busy admiring her new hat they'd forget to stare at the red welt around her neck, because today was the first time she would go out in public without her bandages. The past week, they'd been covering nothing but a scar but she couldn't give them up. Not until this morning, when she realized she was using them as a crutch, and Garnet Diana Dulan did not need a crutch. She was made of steel and barbed wire, she'd reminded herself as she took the bandage off and tossed it aside.

She was half an hour early for services so she could practice the hymns Matthew had said they'd sing that morning. The small church cemetery lay right behind the church house building. When she passed it she wondered about the crosses there. The town was only a few years old, the area being settled at first by the silver miners. Sometime when she had more time she'd wander among those who'd been buried there to discover a little more history of Frenchman's Ford. She'd heard that there were volumes of history books in every cemetery.

The doors squeaked when she opened them and a blast of musty air hit her in the face. "Yuck," she said, hurrying to open the windows to let the fresh morning air into the church before the congregation arrived. She opened the hymn book to *Amazing Grace*, pulled out the bench, and fluffed her skirts, wiggling until she was comfortable. A moment later she began to play the first verse, softly like a prayer. The music filtered through the open windows and up and down the streets of Frenchman's Ford, maybe not as resounding as a big brass bell would have done, but calling the citizens of the town to morning services just as well.

Stella Nash was the first one to make her way through the doors. She stuck her aristocratic nose straight in the air when Garnet nodded at her. She'd most likely be in a snit for a month since her temperance saloon smashing plans had gone awry the night before. She took a seat on the front left pew and folded her hands in her lap. There was a cold steel rod that extending from her tailbone to the top of her skull, Garnet was sure. Simple bones could never hold up any woman's body that rigid without help.

Garnet turned to *"Abide With Me,"* and let her fingers trill over the fairly new hymn. Ruby Ann and Cletus were the next members to arrive. Stella stuck her nose even farther in the air. Garnet bit the inside of her lip to keep from smiling. Stella blamed Ruby Ann for the whole failure. She'd accused Ruby Ann of telling Cletus about their plans to attack the saloons. It was the only way in the whole world Sheriff Gabe Walker could have found out, according to the fit she'd thrown. Ruby Ann wore a new calico shirtwaist it that fit her round body perfectly and she didn't care a whit what Stella thought. The woman was radical to begin with, and getting just plumb daft every day she lived. She hadn't let the cat out of the bag concerning the saloon bashing and she didn't appreciate Stella's ugly accusations. Lately, Ruby Ann had been having misgivings about all that temperance stuff anyway so she was glad down deep in her heart that Stella had given a reason for her to quit the meetings.

The preacher and his family arrived before Garnet finished all the verses of "*Abide With Me*." He and Betsy both smiled at Garnet and took their places on the front right pew. Betsy had filled Garnet in on the failed temperance gossip last evening when she brought over a loaf of fresh baked bread right about dark. She'd told her to be prepared to pick icicles off certain members of the congregation that morning.

Slowly the pews all filled to capacity, but Garnet didn't miss the last person to sneak in and sit down on the back pew. How could she? Just his presence brought a case of hives to her arms and neck. By sitting up very straight, she could see past Dusty and between Cletus and Ruby Ann, right into his face. He slumped slightly in the narrow pew but he seemed intent on listening to the sermon. She studied him for a long while; the line of his square jaw, that slight cleft, those lips that had stirred up her passions and left her in bewilderment. When he caught her staring, she slowly shut her eyes and turned to focus entirely on what Matthew was saying.

It gave him the perfect opportunity to do some looking of his own. She'd left off the bandage this morning. He could see part of the angry scar above the collar on her dress. He longed to kiss it and make it go away like his mother had done when he was a little boy and had a hurt. Garnet would most likely pluck out his eyes and feed them to desert lizards before she'd let him kiss her ugly scar. The kiss they'd shared was just an accident. When he'd left her place after the earthquake, he'd said good-bye like a gentleman. Her one word answer of "forever" was branded on his heart as surely as if he'd heated up an iron, bared his chest and let Jonah hit him with the hot metal. Garnet Dulan was a woman to ride the river with and someday a man would come through Frenchman's Ford who'd see her good qualities. Whoever he was, he'd darn better keep his britches on twenty four hours a day, though, because if he ever dropped them, she'd snatch them away and wear them the rest of the marriage. Jealousy washed over him when he thought of another man kissing those delectable lips. He shook it off. What Garnet Dulan did was none of his business. He'd ruined any chance he might have had at getting to know her better the day he marched her barefoot across the street and tossed her in a jail cell. He tried to concentrate on Matthew's sermon. Something about minding your own business. He used the phrase, "live and let live," and Gabe figured the words were probably sitting like a red hot coal of fire on Stella's heart if she was listening to a word of it.

Garnet's thoughts wandered back to Stella, too. Anything to get Gabe off her mind that morning. She figured the woman hadn't heard a thing all morning. But then if her plans had been put to naught like hers had been, Garnet would have been ready to blow the bottom out of that commandment "thou shalt not kill." It was evident that Stella's body was in church, but her mind was somewhere off visiting with other unrenowned martyrs. Ruby Ann was nodding in agreement with everything Matthew said and so was Cletus, who was no doubt very glad his wife wasn't part of that radical bunch of women anymore.

When the services ended, Betsy was the first one beside Garnet as she put the lid down on the piano. "So you took off the bandage. It don't look so bad. Why don't you join us at our house for Sunday dinner. We been running in and out of your place these past days and you've not been down the road to see how the Smith family lives. We'd love to have you," she said.

"I haven't made a thing to contribute," Garnet said.

"Then next week you can help me make a hat like that. Is it one of those cheap straw hats down at Dusty's store? I just love it," Betsy said. "If you can make something like that out of a plain old summer straw, I'd love to see what you could do with a man's felt hat for the winter time."

"Deal," Garnet said. "Don't be buying trim for the hat, though. I got lots of bits and pieces. We'll put you one together in no time. There was scrap left from the girls' dresses down at the Silver Dollar so maybe you'd like some satin roses on yours."

"Yes, I'd like that. Now let's get on down the road. You can ride with me and Charity. Matthew can walk home with the boys after he's greeted and talked to everyone. Can't slight a single soul today with feathers ruffled so bad," Betsy said.

"Ain't it the truth," Garnet said, her voice gravelly and low, but at least it had progressed beyond a whisper. She'd asked the doctor in the middle of the week when she went in for him to check the scar if she'd ever be normal again.

"Depends on what you call normal," he'd said. "If you're askin' me if you'll sing soprano, the answer is no. If you're wonderin' if it'll stay just like it is, the answer is yes. You're just lucky to be alive and able to talk at all."

Gabe was walking up the street toward the jail when Garnet and Betsy made it through the crowd to the doors of the church where Matthew greeted everyone in the congregation. Betsy told him she and Charity were going home to get dinner started; for him to gather up the boys and bring them with him. Charity whined that she wanted to stay with her father and visit with her friends.

"Mind your mother," Matthew said seriously. "If she says she wants you to go home then she's got something in mind."

"But Daddy," Charity rolled her eyes.

"No buts, girl," he said.

She didn't say anything else but the set of her shoulders and the way the dust boiled up around her shoe tops when she stomped out to the buggy attested to the fact that she didn't like that answer. Garnet suppressed a smile. She remembered acting just like that when she was Charity's age. Had it really been that many years ago? She could scarcely believe all that had happened since she was a little girl in short skirts and pigtails.

The Smith place was set back in a grove of pinion trees next to the river. The little white-washed house was surrounded by well-tended flower beds. Three big cats lounged on the porch steps, and a swing on one end moved lazily in the afternoon breeze. Peace cradled the whole place like a mother with her first born child. Even before they were out of the buggy, Garnet was glad she'd agreed to the dinner. Betsy told Charity to take the buggy to the barn, unhitch the horses and put them in their stalls. Then she was to come back to the house and help with dinner.

"Bet it don't take her all day to get that job done. She's quite taken with you," Betsy laughed as she ushered Garnet into her home.

"Oh, my," Garnet stood just inside the door and admired what was before her. A living room with a big fireplace. An open door straight ahead with a feather bed testifying that it was the master bedroom in the house. An archway led off to the left into a kitchen with a cook stove and eating table as well as a cook table and lots of shelves. The loft actually had real stair steps leading up to it rather than a ladder affixed to the wall.

"It's lovely," Garnet said.

"We're really glad to have it," Betsy said. "Oh, I forgot to tell you, we always have a guest on Sunday."

Garnet's heart stopped beating then took off like a second grader on his way home after a long day of school: in a dead, all out run. They'd invited Gabe. She'd have to think up some kind of excuse to bow out of the invitation and go on home. Darn it all, anyway. She'd looked forward to a Sunday afternoon with Betsy and the children. She'd have to plead a sudden headache. A lie and on Sunday at that. But she could not bear to be in the house with Gabe.

"Have mercy, honey, you look like you just saw a ghost. I should've told you about our Sunday guest. We can't very well not include him. Not after all he's done for us. Zebediah don't eat right as it is. Mines that silver and eats beans out of cans all week. He's a real humorous old man. He won't never even see that scar so don't get in a panic," Betsy said. "Now the bread is all raised up. You can make out the hot rolls. Floor can is on that shelf," Betsy nodded toward the shelf above the dry sink. "Aprons are hanging beside the back door. The one with red trim is mine. You can lay claim to any of the others."

Garnet bit her lower lip and smiled. Zebediah! She'd been wanting to meet the fellow ever since he gave her a place to live. She'd have to stop letting every other thought involve Gabe. He was most likely already sitting up to the table at Stella's house and getting his ears burned with her fussing. How he could live in that place with that shrewish woman was a complete enigma to Garnet. It was a wonder Stella hadn't thrown him right out on his hind end when he met her at the front of the Silver Dollar and informed her that if she damaged one thing with the club she was toting that he'd be honor bound to haul her to jail. And she would do her thirty days in jail for destruction of public property because he'd see to it no one bailed her out.

"Whatever are you thinking of?" Betsy asked.

"Oh, whether or not Stella is going to pitch Gabe out in the street," Garnet said.

"No, she won't. Gabe is her only full-time, pay-on-time boarder. She might make him miserable but she won't throw him out. Besides if she does, he'll just go back to living above the jail. There's a couple of rooms up there. I understand that when Stella's husband died and she started up the boarding house that Gabe moved over there because he felt guilty. He still has most of his belongings up above the jail, though," Betsy said.

"Hmmm," Garnet said, grabbing each little word about Gabe as if it were a lifeline and she'd fallen overboard. She busied herself so Betsy wouldn't see the scarlet creeping from her neck up to her cheeks.

"Momma, Zebediah helped me get the horses done," Charity came through the door holding an elderly man by the hand.

"Zebediah, meet Garnet. Garnet, Zebediah," Betsy said.

"Right glad to meet you," Zebediah extended his hand. His blue eyes twinkled in a bed of wrinkles and he raised his heavy gray eyebrows when she reached out and shook hands with him.

"Likewise," Garnet said.

"Hey, everyone," Matthew's big voice boomed at the front door. "Hello, Zebediah. Betsy is making fried chicken. That's your favorite, I know. Well as Gabe's. Hey, Gabe come on in. Betsy, we got more company. I talked Gabe into coming to dinner, too. He can't be eating Stella's food today. It might have arsenic in it. Garnet is making rolls, I see, so we should only be about an hour away from dinnertime. You see, I got these things timed real well."

Garnet hands shook so bad she practically dropped the bowl holding the yeast bread dough. She looked up into those blue eyes, filled again with thunder and anger. Great lord! She hadn't set this whole thing up. She'd been willing to fake a headache to get out of it, and then there he was. She narrowed her own aqua-colored eyes and glared right back at him, tension building in the room thicker than smoke in a fiery blaze. The air crackled with sparks flying across the kitchen and into the living room.

"You sure you got enough food?" Gabe said.

"Sure we got enough food," Charity piped up. "Momma wringed the heads of four chickens this morning. She says Daddy eats more than that big old giant in the Bible. She even told him she bet that giant had red hair."

Somehow they got through the preparations and Garnet's heart had stopped fluttering around like pancakes on a hot griddle. She could do this. She'd just sit through the lunch and then make excuses that she had to go home early. She had herself convinced until Charity told everyone where they would sit, and she seated Gabe and Garnet right beside each other.

Garnet laced her fingers together and squeezed tightly. They still shook. She bowed her head and squeezed her eyes so tight that her head ached while Matthew offered the blessing before they ate. The image of Gabe in all his Sunday morning finery did not fade. She inhaled deeply but it didn't erase the tingles playing hopscotch up and down her backbone at the touch of his hip crowded next to hers on the short bench.

Gabe folded his hands in his lap and bowed his head during grace. He would have refused the invitation to lunch if he'd known Garnet had been invited also. His jaws ached from clamping them so tight but the first exasperation he'd felt when he found Garnet in the Smith kitchen had subsided enough that he could breath again. She was beautiful standing there with a faded gingham apron over her Sunday dress. He'd wanted to reach out and brush away that smudge of flour on the tip of her nose, but that would have caused such a ruckus, it would have brought the whole house down around their ears. He knew better than to touch her, ever again.

"Amen, now let's eat," Matthew said, a smile covering his face.

"Daddy, what's a seance?" Charity asked in the quiet moment before everyone found something else to talk about.

"A what?" Matthew asked.

"You know, a seance? Stella said she might have to have a seance and call her dear husband back to tell her whether to stay in Frenchman's Ford or to take herself back to the East where she could do some good against the evil men who go in saloons," Charity picked up the hot rolls and passed them around the circle.

"A seance isn't something you should be thinking about. It's a crazy idea some folks have that has to do with raising the spirits of the dead folks," Zebediah explained, keeping the chuckle down deep in his chest. If Betsy and Matthew could see their own faces, they'd laugh, too.

"Can that really happen?" Charity laid a fried chicken leg in her plate when her brother passed the platter to her.

"Of course not," Gabe said.

"What makes you so sure?" Garnet turned toward him.

"Oh, come on." Gabe loaded one corner of his plate with mashed potatoes and grabbed a hot roll as the plate went past him. "Surely you don't believe that hocus-pocus stuff."

"No, I don't, but I just wondered what made you so absolute sure. Have you sat in on one? Can you actually vouch for the fact there is no such thing?" Garnet asked.

"Aren't the roses pretty this time of year?" Zebediah said, only a slight chuckle in his voice. "You know, Momma would be so glad that we got a piano player in the church now. We come out here to mine the silver. Bought us a stake and Momma made me build that church before we even built the cabin. She'd go there of a Sunday and just sit there on the front pew. I asked her one time what she wasted time like that for and she told me that she was visitin' with God. She listened to a couple of hymns in her mind and then she pretended there was a preacher right up there on the pulpit tellin' her about the Bible. Strange thing was she got some peace from that. She died 'fore any of you good people come along, but she would be proud to have a piano player in there."

Betsy just stared at Zebediah. He'd never talked that much at one time since she'd known him. He had a tremendous sense of humor but usually only spoke in one or two sentences. When he stopped talking everything fell silent for several moments.

"Well," he drank deeply of the water to the left of his plate. "Guess you two children have had enough time now to stop fussin'. Momma wouldn't like that of a Sunday."

"Yes, sir," Garnet said. "I guess we have at that."

"Good lunch," Gabe said.

"Not lunch. It's dinner," Charity said. "We just can't get you raised up proper, Gabe. Dinner is at the middle of the day. Supper is at the night time. Zebediah said you didn't come from no highfalutin bunch of people back there in Kentucky. Didn't they say dinner and supper?"

"Yes, ma'am, they did. Guess I just forgot the way of things," Gabe said, moving slightly away from Garnet so that he didn't touch her. The pressure of her thigh next to his was more than he could bear for another moment. Already visions of slipping his arm around her waist and kissing her right in front of Zebediah, the preacher and even God, were playing havoc with his thoughts.

Garnet moved the other way. If he didn't want to sit beside her he could very well carry his dinner plate out to the yard and eat with the cats. She didn't care if he dropped dead on the spot or if someone put a bullet through his heart on the main street of Frenchman's Ford. Cold sweat broke out on her face when she saw him lying in a puddle of his own blood in the middle of the dusty street. She didn't want him dead. She wanted him to kiss her again. Kiss her until she was breathless.

After dinner was finished, the men went outside to the porch. Betsy gave Charity permission to walk to her friend's house in town. Ruby Ann and Cletus had a daughter just her age and she took off in a dead run.

"Why walk when you can run, even if it is hot and dusty for an autumn day?" Garnet watched out the kitchen window at Charity's skirt tails swaying from one side to the other.

"I got my job cut out making a lady out of her," Betsy said. "So what's going on with you and Gabe?"

"Nothing," Garnet sunk her hands into the hot soapy water and kept her eyes on the dishes.

"Sure," Betsy giggled. "He's besotted. Couldn't keep his eyes off you all during dinner."

"I don't think so," Garnet said.

"Oh, Betsy," Gabe stuck his head in the back door. "Thanks for lunch. I've got to get back to town. See you around."

"You are quite welcome. Garnet is just leaving, too. You can walk her as far as her house," Betsy jerked the apron from around Garnet's waist and slapped her on the shoulder. "When opportunity knocks, open the door and invite it in," she whispered as she sent Garnet out the door and straight into the devil's own lair.

"I'm sorry," Garnet said when they were out of hearing distance. "Single woman. Single man. Every married woman in town gets match making ideas."

"Well, they can just forget it," he said, and could have bit his tongue off. Or whipped his gun from his hip and shot himself right between the eyes.

"That's the gospel truth according to the good sheriff," she said bluntly.

They walked in silence until she could see her own cabin. When they reached the edge of her yard, he tipped his hat and started to walk away. She stomped her foot, dust flying up half way to her waist and settling back down on her best skirt. For that bit of impetuosity, she'd be brushing her skirt for an hour. She turned quickly and stepped in a gopher hole, let out a scream and fell flat on her back, knocking the wind solidly from her lungs.

Gabe heard her scream and was at her side in seconds, gathering her up in his strong arms. He kicked the back door open with his foot and carried her to the bed where he laid her down gently. "Garnet? Can you talk to me?" he asked, worried that she'd hit her head.

She gasped, very unladylike, and sucked air into her lungs several times before she even attempted to speak. "Yes, I'm alive," she said, looking up at him. He was so close the cleft in his chin was out of focus.

"You scared the devil plumb out of me," he almost shouted.

She wished she could do the same, but all she had was a gritty whisper to offer to the argument. At least there was no Zebediah to stop the fight this time. "Good, maybe you'll be nicer," she said.

"You are a witch!" He drug his hands through all that gorgeous thick sandy brown hair.

"We won't discuss what you are," she said right back.

Then his lips were on hers and the cabin felt somewhat like it had when the earthquake hit. The kiss lasted an eternity; it was over in less time than it takes a butterfly to wink. Her hands were behind his neck, tangled up in his hair when they came to themselves.

"Another mistake?" she asked.

"You bet it was," he said. "Just relief that you weren't dead."

"I see," she said. "I suppose you'd better never come in here again. Seems like the bed keeps drawing us together and making us do things we don't want to do. If you stay away, then we won't be making mistakes."

"Good-bye, Garnet," he said, picking his hat up from the floor where it had been knocked off when he came in the kitchen door.

She waved, not trusting her weak voice to say a single word. When he was gone she drew her knees up and locked her arms around them. Had she just fallen in love with the most unacceptable man in the whole of Nevada Territory?

Chapter Eleven

Garnet stood in the deep shadows of the church house and watched Ruby Ann's daughter, Imogene, and Charity light two candles and stick them down in the dirt on top of a grave. The gentle night breeze picked up their whispers and carried them to Garnet but she couldn't understand what they were talking about. She could have gone on back to her cabin now that she'd seen Charity was safe and nothing was wrong with her family, but curiosity kept her glued to the outer wall of the church.

Not fifteen minutes earlier she'd just come out of the outhouse when she thought she'd seen one of Aunt Lulu's ghosts. Closer inspection told her it wasn't someone already gone on to the hereafter but merely Charity Smith with her white nightrail flapping around her legs as she ran down the road. Garnet's first idea was that someone had taken ill and they'd sent Charity for the doctor in town, so she followed the child. Right to the cemetery where Imogene quickly joined her.

"What do you think they're up to?" Gabe said right at Garnet's elbow.

She came nigh to jumping right out of her skin, and would've screamed loud enough to wake the whole town if she'd had a proper voice to do it with. Gabe laid three fingers across her lips and that gesture set her to thinking about his kisses, which created a flash of fury at herself for letting him affect her that way.

"What are you doing here?" she slapped his hand away. Good grief, there she was in her nightrail and a shawl, her hair braided down her back and her work boots on her feet. If anyone saw her with him dressed this way, the gossip would light up all of Nevada Territory by sunrise. Matter of fact, if anyone saw her gallivanting around at night attired like she was, there wouldn't be any need for a sunrise. The gossip would be so hot, it might even just melt the whole state with one big fire ball.

"Followed Imogene. I was sitting in the jail when I saw her go sneaking past in her nightgown. Figured she might be going for the doctor or something so I followed her. This is where she led me," he leaned forward and whispered softly in her ear.

She gathered the shawl tightly around her shoulders and hoped he accredited the shivers to the night air. "Me, too. I followed Charity for the same reason. I was coming out of the . . . well, I'd been out back when I saw this white thing floating down the road. For a minute I thought I was seeing one of my auntie's ghosts."

"I think they're setting up a seance." He pointed. They'd joined hands and were circling the candles, their heads thrown back looking up to heaven as they chanted something neither Gabe nor Garnet could understand at first.

"Oh, great one in the sky, if you could just let Zebediah's beloved come and talk to us, we'd be obliged," Imogene finally piped up in a loud clear voice. "Zebediah wants to know if she can hear Miss Garnet play the piano on Sunday morning."

"And if you could just send me Stella Nash's husband, Mr. Joe Nash," Charity said as serious as a preacher on the last night of revival, "We need to get him to tell us to pass the word on to her that it's okay for her to go back East even though his body is buried here in Nevada Territory.

Carolyn Brown

That's what we want, great one in the sky. We need to talk to these two dead people so we can help take care of our town. Zebediah is worrying, and Stella is worrying the whole town with her rascal ideas."

"I think she means radical," Garnet said.

"Radical. Rascal. About the same far as I'm concerned," Gabe had trouble keeping the laughter inside. The scar around Garnet's neck was very visible but it sure didn't take away from the beauty of her standing so close to him he could smell the soft rose water she must have bathed in. He could still hear his mother telling him to keep his hands behind his back so he wouldn't touch things he wasn't supposed to. Unconsciously, he put his hands behind his back. He clasped them tightly so he wouldn't take the ribbon out of the end of that braid and tangle his hands in all her gorgeous red hair.

The little girls continued circling and chanting, "Come down and talk. Come down and talk."

Garnet stifled a giggle. Gabe didn't do so well. He slapped his hand over his mouth but the chuckle came out like a great owl's hoot. Both girls stopped, took one look at each other, let out a scream that should have opened every grave there and took off like greased lightning toward their homes.

"You follow Imogene and I'll make sure Charity gets home without having a heart attack," Gabe said.

Garnet nodded. Anything to get away from the effect of having Gabe so close to her side. Imogene had her gown tail hitched up and her chubby little legs were a blur in the light of the full moon as she ran down the sidewalks and toward her house a few hundred feet from the lumber business. Garnet saw her slip inside the front door and imagined her sliding down the backside of it to get her nerves in control before she went sneaking up the ladder to the loft. Ruby Ann would have her scrubbing floors and windows for a week if she found out what the child had been up to that night, so she'd better be very, very quiet as she made her way up to her bed. Garnet silently wished her the best of luck.

Garnet waited a few more minutes, hidden in the darkness between the Spur and the jail house before she turned around and started back home, giggling the whole way. The quietness of the town was eerie that late at night, but she wasn't afraid. Not even when she took time to open the gate in the white washed picket fence surrounding the cemetery. She marched up to the grave which had a cross bearing the name of Nadine Jones, beloved wife of Zebediah Jones, and plucked the candles out of the dirt. She blew out the flames, and carefully filled in the holes so no one would ever know the girls had been out there trying to call down ghosts from the great one in the sky.

"I know you like the idea of someone playing the piano in church," she whispered to the cross. "You don't have to visit me and tell me in person or ghost or whatever they wanted."

She walked slowly down the road to her cabin. The night air was cool and the moon was absolutely beautiful. Deep in thought when she turned into the yard, she didn't see Gabe sitting on her back porch. Not until he cleared his throat and spoke did she realize she shared the night with anyone else.

"Hello," she said. "Did you get your witch home safely?" For some reason it seemed totally natural for him to be sitting there, leaning against the porch post, his hat in his lap.

"Yes, and you?" he asked.

"Ran the whole way. I think that laugh you tried to hold back probably scared the bedevil right out of them. They only thought they wanted the dead to come back and talk to them," he said.

"You believe in that stuff?" he asked, standing to his feet.

"No, I do not. Aunt Lulu raised me for a while and she did. Lord, she was so superstitious it was just plain frightful. If I can't see it or touch it, I don't believe in it," Garnet brushed past him on the way in the house.

"Sit with me a while," he motioned to the other side of the porch. "I'd like to talk."

"Oh?" She cocked her head to one side. "And what on earth would we have to talk about Gabe Walker? The friction between us?"

"For starters," he said. "Come, sit down for a while. I don't know much about you, Garnet Dulan."

"And why would you want to know about me? So you can run me out of town?" she asked caustically but she did sit down.

He joined her, leaning back on the post again and enjoying the view. Garnet's lovely face was half in shadow; half lit up by the full moon light. She'd drawn her shawl tightly around her shoulders, and the her body language said she'd rather be anywhere but on the porch with him.

"No, I just thought since we'd been thrown into this situation we might talk a while. You don't want to?" he paused.

"I want to," she said honestly. This was so different from teenage flirtation, yet her heart fluttered around just as wildly as it did when she was a young girl and the boy of the day paid a bit of attention to her. "I don't know much about you either, Gabe. So why are you in Frenchman's Ford?"

"Zebediah's wife was my mother's aunt. She and mother kept in touch when Aunt Nadine and Uncle Zeb came out here. It sounded so exciting to go West and mine for silver. Aunt Nadine wanted family around her and since they didn't have kids, Uncle Zeb had kind of adopted me. Anyway, one day a letter came to Momma, only it was addressed to me. Aunt Nadine said she wanted me and Jonah to come to Nevada Territory. Jonah laughed and said he'd go with me if he could own a saloon. So Uncle Zeb built the building for us, gave me a fourth and Jonah the rest. Then he marched me down to the city meeting and they hired me on as the sheriff the week after I got here. Uncle Zeb would finance anything I wanted but I want to make it on my own. I'm twenty-eight years old and been here three years. I've saved enough to invest in the new stamp mill going in next spring, too," he said.

She let that soak in a few minutes. Adventure. That's what Stella said her husband was seeking in Nevada Territory, too. But what would happen when the adventure was over, when the town was settled and boredom set in? Would Gabe Walker ride out of town like Jake Dulan had done? Or when Zebediah went on to meet Aunt Nadine in eternity, would Gabe take his inheritance and disappear?

"Think you'll stay around?" she asked.

"I don't know. For a while I thought about going on to California to look into a gold mine. Uncle Zeb says he'll grubstake me if I want to go, but right now Frenchman's Ford is still pretty rough around the edges. And there's not a lot of years left in Uncle Zeb. I want to spend as much time with him as I can. I've got a lot of work here, and besides I'm buying into so many things that my roots are going deep," he said. "How about you, Garnet? Why didn't you go on with that wagon train of brides bound for California?"

"Because I never intended to go all the way to California. Not even when Willow talked me into putting my name on the line. I told them I'd go but I wasn't marrying any man I didn't love. There's five of us Dulan sisters, but until last April we all thought we were the only child Jake had. Crazy idea, ain't it? He was a young man back when we were born but no one in our families talked about him much. Anyway, we each got a letter from him saying he was on his deathbed and wanted to see us before he died. He didn't get that wish granted. He was dead when we arrived. Willow came from Pennsylvania. Gypsy from south Texas. Velvet from North Carolina. Gussie from Tennessee and I came from Arkansas. We met at the church and then Rafe Pierce read the will after the funeral. That's when we re-

alized we were sisters. Anyway, Jake had left us room and
board for a week. Looked pretty bleak there in St. Jo, Missouri until Willow got it in her mind we'd join up with the
wagon train Jake was supposed to be helping Hank take to
California."

"What happened to the other sisters? They go on?"

"No, Willow and Rafe got married. The one who read
the will to us. He was hired on to help with the wagon train
up into Nebraska. Then just outside of Fort Laramie, Wyoming, Velvet came down with a horrible fever. It killed
another woman but Patty O'Leary took her to the fort, left
her with a doctor there and she lived. She wound up married to that doctor. Then Gypsy Rose left the train to marry
Tavish O'Leary, that would be Patty's nephew, in Utah. It
was just me and Gussie then and it looked like there was
going to be plenty of women to make up the hundred they
needed at the end of the line, so when we got to Frenchman's Ford, I told Hank I wanted to buy back my contract.
He said he hadn't let the other Dulan girls buy theirs back.
He'd just given it to them, so Bobby, that was our Indian
scout, drove me into town and set my truck on the sidewalk
outside the Silver Dollar. You know the rest," she said.

"Why didn't you know about each other? Didn't Jake let
you know when you were children?" he asked.

"Jake married Gussie's momma and she died having
Gussie. He gave the baby to his in-laws and disappeared.
He married my momma next and she got bit by a snake
when I was tiny. He took off again. He never sent word of
any kind. We didn't know anything about him except that
he had blue eyes like ours and that he'd taken off when
our Mommas died. At least four of us, that is. Said in his
will that all he wanted was sons and all he got was daugh-
ters. All the way until Willow. He said that he married her
momma and had give up hope on ever having a son. Sure
enough she was a girl and when she was a year old, he and
Willow's momma found they just plain didn't like each

other. She took Willow and went to Pennsylvania and Jake gave up on marrying any more."

"That's quite a story. You got family anywhere?" Gabe asked.

"Got aunts, uncles, cousins scattered all over the Ozark Mountains. I was shuffled amongst them my whole life," she said.

"You going to stay in Frenchman's Ford, then?" he asked.

"Why? You planning on buying me a ticket anywhere I want to go even yet?" she asked right back, but her voice held humor instead of sarcasm.

"No, that opportunity has long since passed," he said.

"I don't know. I like it here. Love Betsy and the Smith family. The girls at the Silver Dollar are giving me business with their fancy dresses. Women in town are coming around to get me to sew for them, too. Seems like I'll never play a bar piano again and that's what I like, but changes come and I'm not a little girl anymore. I might stay. Guess it depends?" she said.

"On what?" he held his breath.

"On whether I'm happy. I'll stay right here one day more than I'm happy. Figure that's how long it would take me to pack up my trunk and buy me and Thunder a ticket out of here," she said.

Happy. What would it take to make Garnet happy? She hadn't found it on the wagon train or she'd still be on it. Frenchman's Ford hadn't been good to her in the beginning, but here she was. Was there hope that something here was making her happy? Evidently so, since she was still there and hadn't bought a stage coach ticket. Gabe longed to reach out and push that errant strand of red hair back away from her cheek, but would that make her unhappy? How on earth would he keep her happy? Because he sure didn't want her to go anywhere right now.

"It's getting late," she said after several moments of

comfortable silence. "I've got a full day tomorrow in front of that sewing machine in there. I reckon I'd better be going inside."

"Thanks for sitting with me," he stood, set his hat on his head and offered her his hand.

She took it, knowing that the shock would shoot all the way to her sockless toes crammed down into her work boots. When she was standing, the moon lighting them both up, he bent low and kissed her fingers.

"Good night, Garnet," he said. "Maybe I'd better go by the cemetery and take care of those candles."

"Good night, Gabe," she said. "The candles were burned down to nubbins, but I blew them out and filled in the holes. Tossed the remnants of the candles in the brush."

"Good," he smiled, his straight, even white teeth glistening by the light of the moon.

She let herself in the back door and slid down the back of it, much like she'd imagined Imogene doing. Only the little girl was trying to chase the fear of ghosts away.

And you are chasing away what? Ghosts of the past? One's called fear and the other mistrust. Sitting on the floor, trying to shake the goose bumps from her hand where he'd kissed it, she sighed deeply. He'd said goodnight, not good-bye. Was there a bit of hope for a future there? And if there was, did she want it? Could he erase her mistrust of all men? Could he ease the fear that she would be just like Jake and once a family was started, she'd just walk away and never look back? It would take a big man to fill those boots and she didn't know if Gabe Walker could do it.

Gabe touched his lips softly. That red haired woman had an affect on him like no other woman had ever had. But he was trying to build a town and carve out a place for himself and future generations of Walkers. Could he ever even think about a future with a woman who'd played a piano in a bar? Would she ever really be accepted as a decent woman in Frenchman's Ford? Or would the gossips ruin them with their talk of the sheriff courting a woman who'd been hung and who'd made her living in a bar?

"I don't care what people say," he said stoically.

Deputy Les was out for a short stroll before he turned in for the evening. His wife had been teaching their five children the school lessons, and he'd heard multiplication tables until he was sick to death of it all. They'd finally all gone to bed, including his wife who was fussing about the desperate need for a school teacher. Les needed one more cigar before he went to sleep and his wife was adamant about those smelly things in her house. He peeked in the window at the jail. The lamp was lit but Gabe wasn't sitting behind the desk. Probably out back, he figured as he puffed on the cigar.

The evening was pleasant as he passed Stella's place. He crossed the street and started down the other side when he changed his mind and kept walking down the side street. The full moon cast a glow on everything but he was looking at the cabin where Garnet lived. The glow flowing out the windows of her cabin attracted him far more than the moon.

Now there was a woman who should've been run out of town for sure. Sewing for those loose women at the Silver Dollar. Next thing a body knew she'd be sewing for Jezebel's women, too. And they just let her play the piano in the church like she was an angel or something.

He stopped dead in his tracks when he looked up and saw Gabe and Garnet on the back porch, silhouetted by the silvery moon. Gabe bent over her hand and kissed it. The deputy's eyes came near to popping right out of his head when he realized Garnet was wearing her nightrail with nothing but a shawl over it. So that was the way it was. They only sparred in public to fool the good citizens of Frenchman's Ford. But it was darn sure evident they were doing other things after dark. She wasn't one bit better than Jezebel, and they didn't open the doors of the church to Jezebel and tell her she could play the piano.

Les turned and practically ran back to his house.

The next day the whole town knew what he'd seen.

Chapter Twelve

Thunder played with a long skinny, shiny piece of fabric Garnet had tied to the rung of the rocking chair. Every time she batted the ribbon like fabric the chair rocked and kept it wiggling for her. Garnet pinned her hair up, donned one of her faded dresses from the wagon train days, and stretched a length of satin out on the bed to make a third fancy dress for Rosy. This one Rosy had ordered done in black with bright red lace. The other girls had each caught on to the idea and wanted a black one also, each done in their own signature color of lace.

She measured the neckline of the dress, doubled it and cut that much lace from the bolt. She'd barely sat down at the sewing machine when the heavy knock came to the front door. Forsaking the toy, Thunder made a dive for under the bed. She wasn't taking a chance on another shaking house catching her in a position where that big rocking toy could fall on her.

Garnet laid the red lace aside and peeked out the window. "Oh my," she exclaimed when she saw her porch overrun with women. Did they all want something sewn up before Sunday? Betsy was among them so maybe they'd come to be fitted for choir robes. But the church was so small they all sang the hymns. They didn't even have a proper choir like she'd seen in Little Rock when she and Aunt Lulu visited the big church that one time.

"Good morning," she greeted them as she opened the door.

"Don't you play goody goody with us, Garnet Dulan." Stella Nash was at the front of the ranks and had evidently elected herself the general of the forces by the look on her face.

"And you would be talking about?" Garnet's feathers ruffled up in automatic defense.

"We don't have to explain one thing to you," Mary Watkins said. "You're the one who's got explainin' to do."

"About what?" Garnet asked, not even thinking about the night before. Surely these women weren't on the war path because she was continuing to make fancy dresses for barmaids. They'd known that from the beginning. She hadn't tried to hide one thing about what she sewed, even if it wasn't one bit of their petty little businesses.

"Garnet, just tell us why you were entertaining Gabe Walker so late last night," Betsy said softly. The women had all come to her house that morning so soon after breakfast that she didn't even have the dishes washed. They'd marched in and demanded that she go with them to confront Garnet about her flagrantly slapping the whole town in the face when it had been good to her. Didn't they look the other way when she actually let those barmaids come to her house? Betsy had reminded them that Dusty didn't turn them away from his general store and what Garnet did was just business. They didn't see the barmaids coming to her house for tea and cookies, did they? But they'd insisted she come with them, and down deep inside her heart, Betsy knew that there was an explanation as to why Gabe was on her back porch. Just like there was one why she was meeting a man in her nightrail. None of it made a bit of sense to her, but she'd be glad to have it cleared up.

"I think you'd better state your problem." Garnet glared at the bunch of them, Betsy included.

"We know you was letting him out the back door real late last night. You was wearing nothing but your night clothes and you let him kiss you on the hand," Stella bowed up to her.

"And you want to know what happened before the kiss? All the details?" Garnet asked, her voice low naturally and even lower with pent up emotions.

"That's why we're standing on your front porch," Stella said. "I noticed you didn't invite us all inside like you do him every time he comes sniffing around your door."

"I don't think I've had time to invite you all in, nor do I think I want to now," Garnet said honestly.

"Well, start talkin'," Stella said.

"I don't have a thing to say," Garnet said. "You see what I do is my business. It's none of yours. Not any of you," she stared right at Betsy who blushed. "I make my own money. I play the piano in church for my rent and I don't owe you an explanation for what I do in my own time. Even if I was so inclined to share with you the events of last night I wouldn't now, not with the nasty, petty attitudes you've brought with you."

"Then you're saying you been letting him come here and sleep with you?" Mary gasped.

"I didn't say that. I said what I do is my business and none of yours. Now if you self-righteous ladies will excuse me I've got work to do," she started back inside the house.

"You sorry excuse for a woman. I'll see to it you don't play no more piano in our church and I'll see to it you ain't got a place to live by nightfall," Stella snapped.

"Why, Mrs. Nash," Garnet smiled beautifully. "That would be the pot calling the kettle black now wouldn't it? Your bedroom door is right across from Gabe Walker's and not one soul asks you if you're ever caught in the hallway in your nightrail and shawl, now do they?"

"You'll be on the next stage out of Frenchman's Ford," Stella shouted, pointing her finger at Garnet.

"We'll see," Garnet said. "Good-bye, ladies. Please don't bother me again."

Garnet's heart broke in half after she slammed the door. To think that she and Betsy had been such close friends all these weeks and that it had accounted for nothing when the vicious gossip traveled like wild fire through town. Tears streamed down her face and her body shook with sobs. She'd trusted Betsy just like one of her sisters. Thunder padded out from under the bed and jumped into her lap, expecting Garnet to pet her while they rocked together, but Garnet ignored the cat and cried until she got the hiccups. Thunder was sleeping by then so Garnet laid her gently on the fluffed up feather pillow at the head of her bed. She went back to the sewing machine and ran a gathering stitch down the lace and went back to work. She'd gotten it basted on the neckline of the black satin dress when she heard the next knock. This one not nearly so heavy.

She opened the door just a crack so she could tell who-ever was there, including Betsy, that she wasn't welcome. She didn't have to explain to any of them what she and Gabe were doing on her back porch, but she sure wasn't telling Betsy the story. She wouldn't cause Charity to get into trouble for anything. Not even her own reputation.

"Good mornin', Miss Garnet," Zebediah smiled brightly. "Understand you got some troubles with the women in town. Mind if I come in for a little while?"

Garnet opened the door the whole way and hoped he gave her a couple of days before he evicted her. She needed to at least finish Rosy's dress she had started.

Zebediah took the rocking chair. "You know sometimes I miss this little cabin. Built the one up by the mines just like it, but Momma's spirit ain't in it like it is in this one. Now you want to tell me what happened here last night that has got them women all in an uproar?"

Garnet sat down on the floor between him and the cold fireplace. "If I do you can't tell a soul, Zebediah. Not even

Betsy and Matthew. If they tell me I can't play the piano in the church no more, you can't even tell them then."

"Well, I 'spect that's fair enough, but it's not their call. It's mine. You see, I own that church building and I don't charge them a dime's rent. Town needs a church if we're ever going to be a place for real folks to come and live in. Own the school too, but we can't find a teacher just yet. Like I said, it's my call about you playing that piano. It's the citizens of this town's rights to come or stay home as they please," Zebediah said.

"Then why don't you come?" Garnet asked.

"I do. I just don't come inside. Can't stand that many people all crowded around me. So me and God, well we just have our own visit outside the window. Him and me, we sit there on the grass or on a log when it's cold weather. I can hear the piano and look across the yard to the place where Nadine is. It's like we was in church together that way. Now you want to tell me what's happened between you and my nephew?"

"Nothing happened last night except that he kissed me on the hand and someone evidently saw it," Garnet said, then went on to tell him the rest of the story about the two little girls.

He laughed until he had to take his snowy white handkerchief from the pocket of his bibbed overalls. "Them girls. Ain't that the funniest thing you ever heard. Momma would have liked that story. Why don't you tell the women that so they'll leave you be?"

"Because I wouldn't get those little girls in trouble for anything. And besides it's none of their business, Zebediah. What I do is my business. If I start explaining every move I make now to those women, I'll be doing it the rest of my days in Frenchman's Ford. It will give them power over me, and I'm not willing for it. You think they're going to go jump in the middle of Gabe Walker about why he was here? No, they won't. They'll just say that he's a man and men folks have a different standard than women. I may not crawl up on the temperance box like Stella, but it's not right. And I'm not going to lower myself to give them an explanation," she said.

"You sound just like Momma," he chuckled. "She would have liked you, Garnet Dulan. She would have liked you a lot. You and her, why you could've set up to coffee and ginger cakes and fixed everything in the world."

"I don't know about that," Garnet drew her knees up and locked her arms around them. Zebediah was the wisest man she'd seen in her lifetime. Why couldn't God have given her to him and Nadine to raise rather than Jake Dulan?

"Well, I'll be on my way now. I'll expect to hear you playin' *Amazing Grace* on Sunday. That was Momma's favorite."

"Tell me, how did you know about this so fast? Did Stella really come to the mines to spread the story?" Garnet stood up and walked him to the door.

"No, I came to town for supplies today. She caught me on the street and commenced to telling me what I would and would not do. And Garnet, next chance I get I intend to have a talk with my nephew. Kissing you on the hand when them lips was right there in front of him. I'm plumb ashamed of him," Zebediah laughed and left Garnet standing in the door, her face as red as fire.

Les Watkins carried a smug little grin with him to work that morning. The woman would be gone by the end of the week. He'd be willing to bet his deputy's star on it. Then the men in town would stop teasing him about letting his prisoner get kidnapped, then leaving her for dead when the bandits hung her because he was afraid to touch a dead person. Yes, sir, Les had sure enough taken care of the problem.

"What are you grinning about?" Gabe asked when his only deputy swaggered through the door.

"Stella didn't tell you?" Les asked.

"I didn't go to breakfast this morning. Went down to the saloon and had coffee with Jonah. He and I go over the books on the first of the month," Gabe said. "What's going on?"

"Well, maybe you better tell me what's going on?" Les said authoritatively. "You're the man with the answers. Seems to me after that big mistake you made you'd be taking your business outside of town to Jezebel's place, though. Maybe you just like making one mistake after another. Mayhap it could be, you'll be cashing in your chips and riding out of town if you keep making them mistakes, though. Frenchman's Ford wants a sheriff who's a law abiding *moral* man."

"And I'm not that?" Gabe asked, narrowing his eyes into mere slits.

"You was. Don't think you still are," Les said.

"Mornin'," Zebediah slung open the door and marched inside the jail. "Les, would you mind checking on the town and giving me a few minutes with my nephew. We go over things on the first of the month."

"Seems to me like," Les hitched up his guns and puffed out his chest, "that you're too busy to be a sheriff on the first of the month. Maybe you'd better step down and let a moral man have this job."

"What's happened this morning that I don't know about?" Gabe asked, bewilderment all over his face. "Have I been fired? Did you come for my badge?"

"Les was out for a stroll last night, pretty late. He happened to see you and Garnet Dulan on her back porch. Seems the moon just lit you up like it was daylight. Her in her nightgown. You leaning over to kiss her hand," Zeb said.

"And?" Gabe asked.

"He went home and told his wife who told everyone in town. The woman formed up an army and went out there to insist Garnet tell them what happened. She refused. Said it wasn't none of their business. What she did was her business," Zeb said.

"Well, I'll just go tell them the truth," he said.

"Imogene and Charity?" Zeb's old eyes twinkled.

"They'll get into trouble but they're two little girls. We're talking about a woman's reputation, here, Uncle Zeb," he said.

"You ain't going to say a word. I been to the cabin and me and Garnet just had us a talk. She's right and they're wrong. I'm standing beside her on this. If you say a word, I'll be disappointed in you, Gabe. Give them little girls time to come forward and when they do all them women will be set on their ear," he said.

"They might not," Gabe said.

"Might not. Even if they don't it ain't one bit of this town's business what you or Garnet do on your own time, now is it?" Zeb said.

"But nothing happened. Why didn't she simply tell them the story?" Gabe asked.

"Because it's none of their business. Whether she's innocent of letting you into her bed or whether she's guilty, that's none of their business. Not really," he said.

"I think I'm following what you're saying. There's a double standard for women and men and there shouldn't be. Those women didn't come in here about to skin me and I was the one kissing her hand, so I'm not in as much trouble as she is." Gabe ran his ran fingers through his hair. "I didn't expect to have to fight these kinds of battles when I pinned this star on my chest."

"Don't expect you did," Zebediah got up on his short, bowed legs and tucked the bottom of his overalls into his boots. "And next time Garnet Dulan and you have a little midnight rendezvous, son, for goodness sake kiss her right on the mouth. She and you both will get hung for a lamb as well as a sheep, and a real kiss is a lot more enjoyable than a dry one on a woman's hand."

He waved at the door, but Gabe couldn't say a word. He was totally speechless.

Garnet felt better when she'd unburdened her heart to Zebediah. That along with the knowledge that he wasn't going to throw her out of the cabin, and the fact that he was indeed listening when she played on Sunday, brought comfort to her heart as she went about the task of finishing the dress for Rosy. She'd no more than got the last of the buttons sewn on by hand when someone knocked on her door.

"Guess they're coming back with the rope to hang me again," she said to Thunder as she made her way across the wood floor. "Bad thing is I'm as innocent now as I was when they really stretched that noose around my neck."

Gabe leaned against the door, his hat in his hands when she eased it open, ready to dodge bullets or outrun Stella with a noose in her hands. Her mouth went dry; everything in her brain turned into mush.

"Good evening, Garnet. I've come to ask you to take a few minutes from your job and take a stroll with me. I expect when a woman is self-employed she might do that, huh?" He said.

She wondered exactly what he had in mind. There was thunder in those blue eyes again and a stroll with her down the streets of town sure wouldn't endear him to the citizens. "I think you'd better come inside and we'll talk about this," she said.

"No, ma'am, I will not cross your threshold again. Just sitting on your back porch has caused you enough pain and heartache. I will not be party to any more. I simply want to take a pleasant afternoon walk with you," he said. "So if you will get your shawl and your hat, we could be off. I'll wait on the swing."

She had a refusal on the tip of her tongue. An excuse about not having supper yet and needing to cut out another dress. But it wouldn't materialize. She simply nodded, reached for her hat and shawl, both on the peg beside the door, and stepped outside. "You sure this is wise? You'll have a scar that matches mine by tomorrow if you are seen in public with me. Don't you know I'm a fallen woman?"

He just smiled but the thunder didn't leave his eyes. "If you are a fallen woman, then I must be a fallen man." He offered his arm and she slipped hers into the crook, not one bit surprised at the feeling it evoked down deep in her.

"Ah, a free thinking man. The next thing you know Stella will have you bashing saloons with her," Garnet said.

"I don't think so," Gabe chuckled.

When she looked up at him, she noticed the laughter had not reached his eyes.

They passed the church where Betsy was about to go inside to clean for Sunday morning services. Her eyes were red and swollen but she didn't speak to Garnet. Charity hung back behind her mother, her eyes as big as dinner plates, pleading with Garnet silently not to tell on her. Gabe tipped his hat and spoke to both of them. They nodded in return.

Les puffed out his chest in front of the jail when they strolled by there. He'd have the sheriff's job in a week. He knew it in his heart and then everyone could pat him on the back and tell him what a wonderful man he was, instead of teasing him about not touching a dead body. Gabe Walker was a crazy fool for actually acting like he was courting Garnet Dulan. Walking right down the street with her like that. Why, he was providing the rope for the citizens to hang him with.

Dusty grabbed his broom and hurried back inside the store when he saw them approaching. He was between a rock and a hard place. He was selling sewing goods as fast as he could get them off the freight wagons these days. He didn't want to lose Garnet's business, but neither did he want to lose the business of the families who bought other things. He couldn't tell those interfering women to drop dead and mind their own business, nor could he let Garnet back in his store if it meant he'd lose their dollars.

The barkeep at the Spur was outside for a breath of fresh air. The noise level inside was about par for Friday night and smoke hung in a gray fog over the heads of the men, playing poker or leaning against the bar deep in conversation. "Evenin', Sheriff. Miss Dulan. Nice evening for a stroll, I see," he smiled. One thing that sheriff had was nerve. Any other man in town would have slunk back in a corner. But the sheriff's nerve was nothing compared to that Dulan woman's. She'd do to ride the river with for sure, and if the sheriff ever looked the other way, there'd be a dozen men standing on her doorstep with flowers in one hand, their hat in the other and ready to fall on one knee and propose to the woman. The barkeep didn't believe for a minute that Garnet Dulan was anything less than a well-bred, Southern lady. He'd been around enough of the other kind in his lifetime to weed out a lady when he saw one.

Garnet and Gabe crossed the dusty street behind a dozen horses carrying silver miners coming to town for some Friday night entertainment. They hitched their horses to the rail outside the Silver Dollar and pushed open the swinging doors. It looked like Jonah was going to have a good night. Just wait until next week when Garnet had all of the girls ready to be decked out in black with different colored lace trim. That ought to bring the miners in by the droves.

At the lumberyard, Ruby Ann and Cletus were both in the window. Ruby Ann turned away quickly to avoid meeting Garnet's eyes. That Sheriff Walker would have to be dealt with at the next town hall meeting. Les didn't have enough brains to run the jail but they could put out word they were looking for a new sheriff. Cletus got busy with a new shipment of nails and didn't glance out again for several minutes.

Garnet itched to go into the Silver Dollar but she didn't

mention it to Gabe. She understood what he was doing even if it wouldn't make a bit of difference. Going into the saloon, even for a minute, to see the girls all come down the stairs at the same time, well, that would defeat the whole purpose of this little stroll. They'd barely gotten past when she heard the roar of applause. She'd missed it, but a smile covered her face when she envisioned the ladies in their fancy dresses.

They proceeded on down the street in silence. In front of the boarding house, Stella had just stepped outside to shake the hooked rug from in front of the dry sink in her kitchen. She gasped when she saw Gabe and Garnet out for an evening walk like any two courting adults.

"You get your things out of my house," she hissed at Gabe. "You are no longer welcome here. Don't you have a bit of dignity or integrity?"

"Yes, ma'am, I surely do. And because I have both, I moved my things out of your house before lunch today. I left the bed unmade since I figured you'd surely want to wash the sheets. My rent is paid up for the whole month but I won't ask for a refund," he said.

"You are despicable," she turned on Garnet.

"Mrs. Nash, you might do well to sweep your own door step before you attempt to clean mine," Garnet said, her voice raspy but filled with humor.

"Now where did you get that line?" Gabe asked when they'd turned the corner back toward her cabin.

"From Aunt Lulu. She used it all the time when folks called her a witch," Garnet said.

"Was she?"

"Who knows? She thought she was. Could see into the future and predict things, she said. Sometimes she got it right. Sometimes she didn't," Garnet laughed.

Even though her giggle was soft, he thought it the most beautiful thing he'd ever heard. They'd reached her back door by then and looking over his shoulder, Gabe could see Les, peeking around the side of the church. Apparently, he was gathering more fodder for the gossip mill.

"Garnet I want to ask you to marry me," he said seriously.

"Why?" Garnet asked.

"Because it . . ." he stammered.

"Gabe Walker, you go on back to your job. Thank you for the stroll. Thank you for trying to do the right thing for the fallen woman in town. Both of them are right noble of you. But I won't marry you," she said.

He didn't know he was holding his breath until it came out in a whoosh. "Why?" he asked.

"If you don't know the answer to that question, then you're not as smart as I've figured you to be," she said. "And don't kiss me on the hand, Les is watching from the corner of the church."

"Okay," Gabe grinned mischievously. He reached out with both arms, took a step forward and before Garnet could blink, had his lips on hers in a kiss that lit up the sky like a glorious sunrise rather than a mediocre sunset.

Chapter Thirteen

A curtain of pure ice fell from the rafters and surrounded Garnet as she played that Sunday morning for the church. Knowing that Zebediah was sitting outside the open window, and that she was truly innocent of all the charges they'd lambasted her with, were the two things that kept her on the bench. She played *Amazing Grace* softly, just for Zebediah and Nadine, as the congregation filed in and shot looks at her meant to make her shrivel up and die right there in the front of the church. Matthew called out the numbers to the hymns he'd chosen and she opened the book to play without practicing for the first time. She had to keep her eyes on the notes and didn't see Gabe slip in the door during the first hymn and take his customary place on the back pew.

After three songs had been sung, a bit less enthusiastic than usual, Matthew took his place behind the podium. He'd prayed hard about this morning's sermon, and God had left him high and dry. He'd tried letting his Bible fall open to where he was supposed to preach. It fell open to Matthew and the verse his eyes lit on said, "Judge not, that ye be not judged." He couldn't preach on that and yet the Lord had shut up the doors to heaven, and Matthew stood before his bickering congregation with nothing to offer.

"Daddy," Charity stood up in the front pew. "I got something to say before you go preaching your sermon this morning."

"Oh?" Matthew was almost glad for the reprieve. Maybe God was using Charity to open up the door to what he was supposed to say.

"Me, too," Imogene piped up from beside her mother and father in the middle of the church. Ruby Ann fussed in whispers to her daughter to sit down and be quiet, but Imogene pushed past both of them and into the aisle, marching resolutely up to the front pew where she joined Charity on the front pew. Holding hands for support, the two little girls moved right up to the front of the church.

"You can sit over there," Charity pointed to the pew beside her mother, and Matthew did what he was told.

"We got a 'fession to make," Charity said. "And we figured since you'd all be here on Sunday morning that was the day to do it."

Garnet blinked twice and looked back over the inquisitive looks to see Gabe with a big grin on his face. She noticed a movement in the edge of the window not far from Gabe's pew and saw Zebediah peeking inside.

"It's all our fault the way you women been acting," Imogene said. "Me and Charity decided we was going to have us one of them seance things and call the dead back to life so we could talk to them. So we took us two candles to the cemetery so Zebediah's wife and Stella's husband could see where we was when they come back. We set them on Zebediah's wife's grave and then we held hands and called for their spirits to come on down from Heaven and talk to us," Imogene said.

"We wanted to ask her if she could hear Miss Garnet playing the piano on Sunday morning and if it didn't make her real happy," Charity said. "And if we could get Stella's husband to tell us that it was all right for her to leave town and go on back to the East where she could be a real big person in the temp'rance stuff, then we'd make them both happy."

Ruby Ann and Cletus were both scarlet with shame. Betsy and Matthew had trouble keeping their mouths closed and not gaping wide open in surprise. Both Imogene and Charity knew they were in for a punishment they surely didn't look forward to, but it felt so good to get the whole thing off their chests.

"So we waited until our folks was all sleeping," Imogene picked up the story line. "And we sneaked out the door and to the cemetery, you see. I was being real quiet and thought I'd got past the jail without Sheriff Walker seein' me, but I guess I didn't. Anyway we was standing there going in slow circles with our heads back and calling for their spirits to come down when we heard this big old noise. Lord, a mercy, I thought that Stella's husband had really started down from the sky so I dropped Charity's hands."

"And I dropped hers," Charity nodded, both girls letting go of the other's hands just like they'd done that night. "We both screamed real loud. I think we wanted them to know we didn't really down in our hearts want to talk to no ghosts. We took off running and I looked over my shoulder one time and all I could see was a bright silver badge a twinkling in the moonlight. I figured it was Stella's husband since he was a deputy and all and that he'd really come right down and was going to talk to me. Well, I ran so fast my legs hurt all the next day."

"And I thought the lady following me was Zebediah's wife," Imogene said. "There she was all floating along in a white gown. I figured her for an angel for sure."

Both girls stopped a few minutes, not knowing whether to go on or not. The congregation sat there, wide-eyed, not knowing what to say or do.

"Way I figure it is this," Charity said. "Miss Garnet must've seen me going to the cemetery, same as Sheriff Walker saw Imogene. They both followed us to make sure we weren't running for help for our families. I think it was the sheriff who sneezed or coughed that made that noise that scared the bedevil out of us. Then they each one took a kid to follow home to make sure we was safe. Probably didn't think about the sheriff following Imogene since she lives in town and he'd be closer to his jail. Or about Miss Garnet following me since she'd be going that way anyway. We didn't give them time to be having a grown-up talk about who to take off after. Me and Imogene was so scared we figured we was for sure going to have to talk to a real ghost."

Betsy smiled and nodded. It all made perfect sense. But why hadn't Garnet stepped up and told the truth? Her conscience pricked her heart until it bled. Garnet wouldn't cause Charity to get in trouble even if it meant her own reputation being torn into shambles. That was a true friend, and Betsy had been so judgmental.

"Anyway, that's what happened, up to then," Imogene said. "I guess the sheriff waited on Miss Garnet's back porch so they could tell each other we were home and safe. I tell you I didn't sleep a wink all night though, I was so afraid that Zebediah's wife was going to walk right through the walls into my house and sit on my bed and commence to talking to me. I told God I'd never burn candles on nobody's grave again if he'd just take her on back to heaven."

"Me, too," Charity nodded.

"And we want to tell Miss Garnet and Sheriff Walker that we are real sorry for the mess we've caused them. 'Course if you all didn't act like a bunch of kids it wouldn't have happened to begin with," Imogene said in a loud voice and pointed to her parents and several others. She was already in trouble. She might as well say what was on her mind. She would never get another chance like this one to do so.

"That's right," Charity raised her chin in a bit of rebellion and took up the banner, expecting her father to banish her to the house any moment. After all she'd caused a problem and she would be punished, she was sure. "If Les hadn't been so ready to get the sheriff in trouble so he could have his job, then he might've seen that Miss Garnet had on her boots. If she'd been inside the house all cuddled up in bed with the sheriff do you think she'd a had her boots on?"

"And," Imogene said before Matthew could make himself rise up off the pew and put an end to his daughter talking like that in church.

"And," she repeated for emphasis, "I don't know what's this big thing about kissing her on the hand is anyway. Last week, Tommy Watkins kissed me on the hand. Just grabbed it after church over there under that little tree and kissed it. Wasn't nothing so special about that. I washed it sixteen times with lye soap to make sure I didn't get no fleas or lice or nothing from him."

"I did not," Tommy yelled from the second pew, where Les and Mary wanted to crawl under the seat.

"Tommy, you are in church. You want God to bring down lightning and strike you dead?" Charity said. "I saw you kiss her and then run fast as you could to grab your Momma's hand."

"Well," Tommy puffed out his chest in anger. "I didn't mean to lie. Why didn't you invite me to the seance? I'm not afraid of no ghosts."

"I believe that's enough, girls," Matthew took the pulpit. "And I've a confession to make. I've wrestled with a sermon all week and because of my own prejudiced attitude toward Miss Garnet, God shut up the doors to heaven to me. I just jumped right on the bandwagon with these women and Les, even told Betsy I wouldn't have her associating with a woman like that. Because of that, God didn't give me one thing so whatever I would've said to you this morning would have been mere words, not a stirring from my heart. I think we've all been guilty of the same. Jesus said, 'Judge not, that he be not judged.' I figure that I've got some apologizing to do from my heart, and I also figure I'd better be doing some repenting for letting my own big ego think it knew all about what was going on. So from this pulpit I'm asking for Gabe's and Garnet's forgiveness and I won't forget to beg for God's when I'm on my knees later tonight. Now I think these girls have been very brave for coming forward and delivering a better sermon than I could today. Not that they won't have their punishments. Miss Garnet if you'll play *Amazing Grace*, I can't think of a better song to end today's services on. And we'll just be dismissed with the song. I don't think a benediction is necessary today. We need some private praying, not public."

Garnet sat on the bench for a long time, letting everyone else leave the church. Not a single soul came forward to apologize to her. She wondered if they were all outside pleading with Gabe to forgive them first and foremost. After all, he was the sheriff and she, just a seamstress who made fancy dresses for saloon girls. It didn't matter that they'd slighted her and accused her falsely, now did it?

Zebediah's wrinkled face popped up in the window right beside the piano. He was grinning so wide that his eyes had disappeared. "Guess those girls brought them to their knees," he whispered loudly. "I told you to give them a few days. Boy, was that a show. Momma would've love it."

Garnet had to smile and in doing so, she jerked herself from the self pity pool she'd been drowning in. What others thought of her shouldn't matter one bit. As long as she could keep things straight with God and the woman who looked back at her from the mirror in the mornings when she combed her hair, that's what was important.

"Yes, it was," Garnet said, getting up with a lighter heart than she'd had since she'd had Bobby set her trunk outside the door at the Silver Saloon. "I've got to do something nice for those girls once the punishment is over. They deserve to be chastised for going out late at night like that. But they also deserve to be rewarded for their bravery in coming forward with the truth."

"Take them for a picnic to the river. Just the three of you. They'd like that. Make them feel all grown up. You know, if folks can see down from heaven, I bet Momma was laughing her head off at that little Imogene thinking you was her ghost. She'd been proud to have you for a daughter," Zebediah said. "Music was almighty pretty today, Miss Garnet. I'm glad you are in Frenchman's Ford."

"Thank you, Zebediah," Garnet said. His face disappeared and she picked up the hymnals, stashed them in the bench and slipped out the back door. The sky was as blue as Thunder's eyes, as clear as Gabe's eyes, too. She straightened her back and went home. If everyone in town made things right with God like Matthew said, then things would be right, whether they ever apologized to her or not.

She'd barely gotten inside the cabin when the first buggy pulled up. She opened the door to find the whole Smith family on her porch. Matthew was the first to say he was sorry and beg her forgiveness. Betsy enveloped her in a bear hug, tears streaming down her face as she begged for forgiveness. When she could wedge between her mother and Garnet, Charity stepped up to ask for pardon for not coming forward sooner. It was that she and Imogene had to decide how to do it, and Sunday seemed the best time. That way everyone would hear them say the same things and no one could go off and tell that they'd said something different.

"Momma and Daddy say I can't leave the house for a whole week, and I've got to pick up potatoes when Daddy plows them up next week. I hate to pick up potatoes more than anything. It gets my hands all dirty. And Momma says I've got to wash all the windows, too, along with whatever else she tells me to do. If I talk back one time then they'll add another day to my punishment," Charity said.

"You deserve to be chastised," Garnet said seriously,

stooping down until she was on the same level with the little girl. "But you deserve a reward, too, for coming forward with the truth when you knew it would cost you. So if it's all right with your Momma and Daddy, I'm going to ask you and Imogene to go on a picnic next Saturday with me to the river's edge."

"Oh, Miss Garnet, you really are a lady," Charity squealed.

"Yes, you are," Betsy said. "Now, come on home with us for dinner."

"No, I think I'll just eat my own bread in my own house today and let things settle," Garnet said.

"I understand," Betsy said. "Can we still be friends?"

"Of course," Garnet said.

"You're a bigger woman than I am," Betsy said. "But I'll work on it."

The next buggy brought Imogene and her parents with the same regrets and essentially the same punishment for the child. Garnet made her the same offer she'd made Charity and Imogene's tear-filled eyes lit up with thoughts of a day with Garnet by herself.

Several other women dropped by during the course of the afternoon, and just as the sun was setting, Gabe showed up on her front door step. He knocked, took his hat off and held it in his hands, and waited by the door, his heart beating worse than it did the first time he went to pick up a girl for a barn dance in Kentucky.

"Well, hello, I thought you might be Stella," Garnet grabbed her shawl and stepped outside. She'd just crawled out of enough hot water to cook her; she surely wasn't inviting another pot full by inviting Gabe into her cabin with no chaperone there.

"She'll be around to tell you she's sorry three days *after* hell freezes over," Gabe said. "Would you sit with me a spell on the swing? Or we could take a walk through town?"

"We can sit," she drew the shawl around her shoulders

and sat down, steadying the swing with her foot until he was settled. His big frame took up enough room that his shoulder touched hers, but she didn't suppose Les was playing spy that afternoon. His wife probably had him firmly by the ear and was yelling loud enough into it to make him shudder.

"Girls put on quite a show this morning, didn't they?" he chuckled.

"Yes, they surely didn't have a problem getting it off their chests once they got started. You had a steady stream of folks stopping by the jail to tell you they're sorry?" she asked.

"Few. Yesterday, Les thought he had my badge all sewed up in a velvet bag. Today he's just pretty content to be the deputy," Gabe said.

"You going to fire him?" She asked.

"No, he's lazy as a slug in the middle of the afternoon, but he's a warm body. Don't no one else want the job after Stella's husband got killed. I got to have help some of the time and Les can fill in the spot," Gabe said.

"That's big of you. I'd have fired his sorry . . ." she almost said a bad word there, and coughed to cover it, ". . . hide and threw him out on the street to beg for mercy."

"No you wouldn't," Gabe looked deep into those aqua colored eyes that kept haunting his dreams. "You wouldn't even save your own reputation by telling them the story for fear Charity would get in trouble."

"No, Gabe. I didn't want her to get into trouble. That's the truth, but I honestly didn't tell them the story because it was none of their business. What I do or don't do is my business," she said.

"Then why are we on the porch?" He asked.

"Because," she smiled beautifully. "It's where I want to be this evening."

"Okay, I'll buy that one. Now, I've come to ask you if I might stop by of an evening and take a walk with you, or if we might take a picnic to the river some time. Of course, you'd have to fix it, since I don't imagine you'd want to eat what Stella would prepare for the two of us. I don't cook too well. Been takin' my meals at the Silver Dollar since I moved out of Stella's place. The girls fix up enough for an extra mouth and I chip in for food," he said.

"If I go into the saloon to talk to the girls, I get branded a hussy, but you can go in there whenever you want. Do you think there'll come a time when that will change?" she asked.

"With women like you in the territory, it probably will," he said.

"And that means?" Her hackles raised in defense.

"It means you are a fine woman, one who will change things, that's all," he said.

"Thank you, Sheriff Gabe Walker. Now would you like a cup of coffee and some ginger cakes? I made them yesterday so they're fresh. Next time Zebediah drops in I want to have some to offer him," she said.

"He can come inside but I can't?" Gabe's voice held a cold cutting edge.

"Yes, he can. And that's my business, too. Sit right here and I'll bring them out. We'll enjoy some refreshments while we talk about how much we look like ghosts," Garnet said.

"Wait a minute," he took her hand and held her back from going inside. "You talked around the issue. I asked if I might come by of an evening to visit with you."

"Why?" she met his eyes and didn't blink. Her hand tingled at his touch, but she didn't pull it away.

"Because I'd like to get to know you better," he said, wishing he had the nerve to just up and say out loud that he'd fallen in love with her. That he admired her courage and spunk and he couldn't imagine life without her anymore.

"If that's the best you can do, then I suppose we might get to know each other a little better of an evening," she said. Something in his eyes said there was more, though, and she sure hoped she wasn't reading things all wrong. Because Garnet Dulan had met the man who'd stolen her heart. The one she'd been waiting on to come along for a long, long time.

Chapter Fourteen

"Oh, Miss Garnet, it's been a wonderful day," Charity sighed dramatically. "It almost makes picking up all those potatoes worth it."

"I had to watch my little brother and sister all week, and do the dishes every night and that's not all. I had to wash all the windows and woodwork in the whole house and Momma even made me do the porch sweeping so the whole town would know I was being punished," Imogene rolled her brown eyes, just as dramatic as her friend.

"I think you should have been punished. Neither of you realize just how dangerous it was for you to be out like that so late at night. But it has been a wonderful day, girls. I'm so glad we've had it," Garnet said.

The week had slipped through her fingers even if it had traveled in a snail's pace for the girls. She'd completed the black dresses for the ladies at the Silver Dollar, sewn up two more shirtwaists for Ruby Ann and had orders for the first dresses from the three girls at the Spur. Garnet had taken a look at them, two brunettes and a blond, all of them with green eyes, and suggested matching dresses of emerald green satin. They'd left it in her hands, saying that they just wanted part of the business that was going across the street to the Silver Dollar.

"I don't know why everyone thinks the two of us going out is such a big bad thing," Charity said. "Nothing ever happens in Frenchman's Ford."

"Ain't that the truth," Imogene said. "Just grown men shootin' each other because they didn't win at the poker tables or got all likkered up at the saloons or two of them fightin' over one loose legged barmaid."

"Imogene!" Garnet gasped.

"It's the truth. When Sheriff Walker gets it all cleaned up, there won't be one excitin' thing going on in town," Imogene said. "And besides, that's what Stella says about those women who work in places like that."

"What about the Indian uprisings?" Garnet asked.

"Oh, them Indians ain't going to bother us none. That Chief Winnemucca, he's a good man, my pa says. He's trying to keep peace," Imogene said.

"What about the young one, who want the white people gone from Nevada Territory?" she asked, trying to make the girls see for themselves that they shouldn't be out late at night.

"They'll never come to Frenchman's Ford," Charity said. "Sheriff Walker would take care of them."

"Oh, my, all that wonderful sweet tea is about to make me wet my drawers," Imogene suddenly piped up.

"Imogene!" Charity raised her voice.

"It's just us girls here," Imogene giggled. "We can say things like that when it's just us girls. I'm going over there in the bushes."

Garnet laid back on the quilt, laced her hands behind her head and watched the last rays of the sun feather down through the few clouds. In her peripheral vision she noticed Charity run toward the edge of the river to skip rocks across the water. Garnet shut her eyes, a smile playing at the corners of her mouth. So nothing exciting ever happened in Frenchman's Ford, did it? Wouldn't those girls be surprised to learn that the most exciting thing in Garnet's life was going on right there in Frenchman's Ford. She'd fallen in

love with Sheriff Gabe Walker, who according to the girls
could fight dragons with his bare hands.

"Gar . . . net!" Charity's scream sounded so desperate
that Garnet jumped to her feet, just in time to see her little
friend yanked up by her long hair onto the horse of an
Indian with a wicked look on his face. Garnet took off in
a run faster than Charity or Imogene had ever done, wishing that she could scream, but what voice she did have had
suddenly dried up inside her chest. The Indians laughed
and pointed at her, circling their horses around the one who
held Charity tightly in front of him. They uttered words she
couldn't understand, but it didn't matter. They'd turn Charity loose or she'd break everyone of their necks and enjoy
the job. Most likely they were friendly, she kept telling
herself as she kept running. Maybe even friends of Gabe's,
who were just scaring Charity. She told herself that right
up until two of them slid from their horses and grabbed
her. She kicked. She hit. She fought. But when two others
joined the fray, she lost. They tied her hands together with
a long rope and slung her up on a spare horse, handing the
ends of the rope to the meanest looking brave in the lot.

"Be still and make no trouble," said a man, barely out
of boyhood. "Or he will kill you. He will tie you to that
horse and ride like the wind. Your flesh will be dragged
from your bones."

"You speak English?" Garnet was amazed.

"I do. I will interpret. I am Daniel. You do not have to
whisper. They don't understand. Do what I say."

Garnet had no choice but to nod.

The boy said something to the man holding the rope and
the whole party rode off at a fast pace. In shock, Charity
began to weep and plead with the Indian holding her to
please let her go. She'd find her way back to town. Not
understanding a word, but recognizing the tone, the Indian
snarled. A whining child. If she didn't hush he would throw
her off his horse and put an arrow through her heart. The
woman, now, that was a different matter. She knew when

to accept defeat. He might even ask Legion for her to take as another wife when they reached the camp.

Charity stopped crying and narrowed her eyes, looking ahead at what Garnet was doing. What was it Zebediah had said about the renegade Indians? The ones that didn't want the white men in their land? She'd only been listening with half an ear to the story that intrigued her little brothers, but Zebediah had told about when they came upon him at the silver mine. He was all alone and he bowed right up to them. They hadn't killed him because they respected courage.

Well, if courage was what it took to get her home in her mother's arms, then she'd show this smelly old Indian some courage. She grabbed the hand holding her tightly and sunk her teeth into the side just below the little finger. Like a bulldog she hung on, even when the Indian was yelling something in his own tongue that sounded like gibberish to Charity. She tasted blood and bit harder. He finally yanked his bloody hand free and threw the girl off his horse. Even though the wind was knocked completely from her lungs, she was on her feet in seconds, running like a hare from a hungry fox. Only to be scooped up after a few yards, into the arms of another man. Evidently it was going to take a lot of courage from a girl to show them she meant business. She kicked him in the shins, slapped his face then doubled up her fist and blackened his eye. She was on her way to giving him a first rate bloody nose when another of the party grabbed her from behind and pinned her arms down to her sides. Even then she managed to get two more solid kicks in on the hurt man's legs, before someone else grabbed her legs.

"Legion says to tie her hands to the rope holding her mother and put her on that horse," Daniel said, keeping his distance from the violent child, then he translated it into the other language. He wanted the girl to know what was happening to her so she would stop fighting them.

When Charity heard English spoken she glared at Daniel.

"When Lucifer gets here, he's going to drag you down to hell's fire and roast you for supper."

"Charity!" Garnet exclaimed.

"He will, Momma," she winked slyly at Garnet. "He will. I swear it. Lucifer is going to eat them. He told me to bite that one and if the blood didn't kill me he would come for them tonight. When they light their campfire, he's going to come up through it and they're all dead men."

"Hush, don't tell all our secrets." Garnet let them slip the girl in the loop made by her arms and gathered her close. "Daniel understands English. He'll tell them."

"I want them to know," Charity yelled. "Daniel, you tell them to enjoy the rest of this day because tonight Lucifer is coming."

Using the Paiute language, Daniel told them what the girl was saying. Some of them laughed, guffawing in great gulps; some of them eyed her curiously; most of them stayed as far away as they could. The man with the bleeding hand and the one with the swollen eye were among the later.

They rode until the moon appeared and then stopped in a thick grove of pine trees to make camp. Daniel told Garnet and Charity that if they didn't try to run, they could walk around for a while inside the confines of the camp. Their hands would remain tied together and later they would be tied to a tree so there would be no escape. If they tried to escape they would be killed immediately. Legion already was complaining that the women were slowing down the renegade party. The braver of the Indians started a camp fire and brought out jerky from their saddlebags.

"I thought you all lived on pine nuts and roots," Charity said as she eyed the jerky, her stomach beginning to rumble. It had been hours since she and Imogene had eaten those last two ginger cakes.

"We would if the white man would stay out of our land and stop cutting down our pinion trees for firewood," Daniel said shortly. "So we steal his cattle and we make jerky from the meat because he eats our agave and food supply. Do you want some of the meat, little girl?"

"I'm Charity and this is Garnet, and yes, we want some of the meat," Charity said. "And some water, too. You don't treat prisoners of war like this. You treat them nice."

"You are not prisoners of war," Daniel said. "You are captives. We will find a good brave to husband your mother and we will raise you like an Indian girl should be raised."

"Why?" Charity asked.

Daniel looked away.

"You are a lyin' desert lizard," Charity said. "You're going to kill us both to atone for what those mean men did to your two little girls. Wasn't it enough that you burned down their store and killed them all?"

"You are just a child. You don't know the Indian ways," Daniel said, walking away from the two women.

"Want to make a run for it?" Charity asked Garnet.

"They'd kill us before we got ten feet," Garnet whispered. "Wait until they sleep. Maybe then we can find a way."

"Okay, Momma," Charity said, a wide grin on her face. "Then I guess I'd better go rustle up some more courage so they won't kill us because we're scared."

"Charity, I *am* scared. Do you think Imogene ran back to town and got help?" Garnet asked.

"Sure she did, Miss Garnet. Soon as she could get her drawers yanked back up," Charity said. She marched toward the fire, her head thrown back in a condescending angle just like she'd seen Stella Nash do when she was addressing the temperance ladies, and defiance pouring from her eyes. Not one of the Indians said a word to her as she reached out to warm her hands, still tied securely together.

"Oh, great Lucifer," she threw her hands in the air and looked straight down into the fire. "Listen to me. I'm calling upon you to come and take these thieving, kidnapping

Indians off the face of the earth. They are going against their great Chief Winnemucca's wishes and the wishes of the white men as well. So grab them by the ankles and drag them down. They'd do all right to keep the fires stoked up, but they're pretty useless for anything else. They can't fight real men. They have to grab women and little girls."

Daniel quietly translated everything she said to Legion, whose eyes got narrower with each word.

"Legion wants to know why you are calling on someone named Lucifer and not your god?" Daniel said from the other side of the fire.

"I wouldn't ask God to dirty his hands taking care of you all. He's much too busy doing good to be looking at a bunch of cowards like you," Charity snapped. "Now leave me alone. Lucifer was telling me that you will all grow very sleepy in a little while. In your sleep he is going to jerk you all to hell and fry you. I asked him to save that Legion man over there for me. I want to rip his heart out and fry it up with onions to feed to my cat."

"Who is Lucifer? I've heard of your god. The man who taught me English told me about your god. But he never mentioned Lucifer," Daniel said, fighting hard against the shiver slithering down his back inspite of the fire's warmth on his face.

"Lucifer is the devil and he's the one who takes care of the likes of you," Charity said, then laughed like she thought a witch would do, in a high cackle that raised goose bumps on most of the Indian's heads.

Daniel turned back to translate the message to Legion, who immediately grabbed his chest. The other Indians, though tired from a hard day of scouting to see where they might steal cattle, held their eyes wide open, fearful of sleep.

Garnet bit the inside of her lip so hard she tasted blood, but she didn't smile. Not even once. If the power of suggestion could link up hands with superstition, then perhaps she'd better give Charity a hand. She joined her at the fire, stretching her hands far out over the flames and letting the warmth penetrate through her.

"Momma doesn't talk, you know," Charity said to Daniel. "Indians just like you grabbed her and she fought them real hard. They hung her in a tree and she asked Lucifer to send fire and burn the rope from around her neck. He did and she lived through it. You can't kill Momma. She's a spirit. Not even a real woman. One minute she'll be here at the fire, the next she'll jump in it and be sucked up to the moon before you can blink."

Good Lord, Garnet thought, *if that child thinks I'm going to jump in the fire then she'd better think again.* But not wanting to spoil the mood, Garnet reached up and jerked open the top of her shirtwaist showing them all the scar, made even redder by the fire's glow.

Daniel translated as fast as he could and silence filled the camp. When there should have been talking, passing the jerky around, enjoying the comfort of a fire, they were all spooked beyond belief. Legion said that the child was crazy and they'd turn her loose at the next white settlement or farm. He didn't want her to bring Lucifer into his camp. The woman wasn't crazy but she might do as a shaman. Especially if she could disappear and reappear like that.

"And now, I'm going to do my fire dance," Charity said loudly, bringing every eye upon her. "If a one of you get in my way, you'll be the first one to fall asleep." She kept her head down, staring at the sand and wondering how to begin. She'd seen her brothers play Indian lots of times and they always began their rain dances by stomping one foot. That seemed as good a beginning as anything and she hoped she didn't get too much rain dance into the fire dance. They might recognize that one. She pulled her skirt tails up and stomped six times. That was the devil's number, near as she and Imogene could figure out from the sermons they half-heartedly listened to on Sunday. Then she began a series of witchy screams as she threw her body

backward and forward and put on quite a show around the
fire, kicking up enough sand to almost put the fire out, and
enough noise to beckon Gabe if he was already out there
just waiting for a chance to save them. When she finished
her dance, she took Garnet's hand and led her back to a
tree, where they both sat down.

"We are ready now to be tied. Lucifer will come later
and burn the ropes from us, but we are ready for you to
do what you must. Oh, and if you look up and see blue
eyes, real clear blue eyes, they belong to Lucifer, so you'd
better scatter seven ways to Sunday if you value your sorry
old dirty hides," Charity said. "Oh, Daniel, tell Legion over
there that I won't really rip his heart out and fry it with
onions for my cat. She don't like onions. I'll just feed it to
her raw."

Daniel translated and Legion stormed off to the rope cor-
ral where they kept the horses. The other Indians laid down
around the fire, but Garnet noticed none of them shut their
eyes.

"Girl, what have you done?" Garnet giggled. "Come
morning when they're all still here and we are too, then
what? Are you going to tell them that Lucifer couldn't take
time away from his poker game to come and fry them?
Besides where did you learn all that stuff?"

"Oh, it's just a story. Me and Imogene try to scare each
other with stories. Besides Daniel said he knew about God.
And hollering for God to help them didn't save those men
they killed and burned in the store. I just thought maybe
they wouldn't know about Lucifer and it would at least
scare them a little bit."

"I think it did," Garnet said. "Look at that bunch of full
grown men. They're afraid to shut their eyes. Matter of
fact, you were so convincing I'm about half afraid to go to
sleep, myself."

"Oh, shut your eyes—Momma," Charity giggled. "Lucifer ain't going to get you. You're going up in a blaze of
glory. Now me, he might get me after all the blasphemin'

I just did. Daddy would skin me for sure, but you gotta
promise you won't never tell it."

"I promise. We get out of here, and honey, I might be
convinced to believe in Lucifer myself," Garnet laughed
with her.

The Indians kept a wary eye on the woman and her child.
In the face of the death, they even laughed. Perhaps that
child did have a devil looking after her. If so, they were
all doomed.

Gabe laid amongst the pinion trees and underbrush and
watched Charity do her fire dance. The girl had gumption,
he'd give her that much. Most normal Indians respected
crazy people as much as they did those with courage. Charity was showing that she had a fair amount of both.

It wasn't easy to lay still until the Indians slept. He
wanted to go in there with guns blazing, rescue Garnet and
Charity and ride away with them. But that wasn't practical.
One man against more than a dozen. No, he'd lay still for
a couple of hours and then try to sneak Garnet and Charity
out of the camp.

His heart had stopped racing when he could actually see
the woman and child and knew they were alive. When Imogene came running into town, her skirt tails yanked up
showing drawers and garters, and yelling something with
tears streaming down her face, he'd thought she was pulling
a prank. When she could catch her breath and tell him that
the Indians had taken Garnet and Charity, cold fear washed
over him. He'd never told Garnet that he'd fallen in love
with her. Sorrow filled his chest. She'd never know that he
literally lived for the evenings when they sat on her porch
and talked about everything from the past to the day they'd
just finished living. How he loved her hair, those aqua eyes
that could see into his soul, even the scar around her neck
that reminded him that he could make big mistakes just
like any man.

He'd grabbed an extra horse just in case he found their

bodies, filled a saddle bag with extra ammunition in the chance he found them and had to shoot every one of the kidnappers and left Les in charge of the jail. He'd drawn a quick map for Imogene showing her the river and asking her which way they'd gone. She pointed north, and he hoped the child hadn't been too scared to really know what had happened. He rode to the river and sure enough there were enough horse prints to show the struggle between Garnet and the abductors. The tracks led north and he'd followed them all the way to the grove of trees. Now he had to exercise patience and if Gabe ever came up lacking in anything, it was patience.

Finally just before dawn, he figured the most of the Indians were asleep and he crept toward the tree where Garnet and Charity were tied securely. Garnet slept soundly but Charity's eyes popped open when she felt his presence. Holding a finger over his lips to insure that Charity didn't yell, he approached them quietly. The kiss he planted on Garnet's lips to awaken her was as soft as a butterfly's wings. She awoke from a dream in a start but didn't make a sound.

He'd reached for his knife, attached to his gun belt, and a hand clamped down on his shoulder from behind. He jerked his head around to see Daniel staring right into his eyes, a pistol in his hands and planted in Gabe's ribs. "Are you Lucifer?" Daniel asked very, very quietly.

"Yes, he is and you're all going to burn. By noon you'll be nothing but ashes," Charity whispered. "Didn't I tell you he'd have blue eyes?"

Daniel dropped the gun. "Let me do this. Don't burn the ropes. You might hurt their hands," he said, grabbing his own knife and slicing through the ropes as if they were no more than a pound block of warm butter. "Take them and go. Now. Don't look back. I'll take care of the rest of it."

"We aren't going," Charity rubbed her wrists, red from the unforgiving rope. "Not until we burn the rest of them."

"You go and I promise we will cut a wide swath around

your town forever. Chief Winnemucca's treaty will apply to your town of Frenchman's Ford. I give you my word," Daniel said, holding up a hand.

"Well," Charity mused. "I suppose that's a deal. We'll shake on it." She stuck out her hand and Daniel shook it firmly.

After the devil, or man, or whatever he was, took the women out into the shadows of the darkness, Daniel went back to the embers of the dying fire, lit a stick and burned the ends of the ropes he'd just cut. When the Indians awoke, he'd tell them that Lucifer sliced the ropes with fire he snapped out of the tips of his fingers. And that Lucifer said if any of them ever came near Frenchman's Ford again, he would truly burn them with fire.

"Oh, Garnet," Gabe drew her close before he gave her a foot up onto the spare horse. "I was so afraid they'd kill you both."

She looped her arms around his neck. "So was I until that imp, Charity, went to work on them."

"Oh, you two, stop mooning around. Those Indians will be awake soon and we need to be down the road," Charity giggled. "Remember you promised, Garnet."

"I'll keep it," Garnet said, and brushed a quick kiss across Gabe's mouth.

When they got back home, she and Gabe were going to have a serious talk and none of it had a thing to do with the Indians capturing her and Charity. They were going to discuss all the things in her heart, and if he felt the same, then so be it. At least she'd have the weight off her own chest.

Chapter Fifteen

Garnet dozed as the horse kept a steady pace with Gabe's, resting her chin on Charity's red hair, so very much like her own. No wonder the Indians thought she was the child's mother. She jerked awake as she began to fall to one side, but before she could get her eyes open, Gabe's arm shot out and braced her back in the saddle.

"I think we'd better stop for an hour," he said. "Eat something. I've got some things in the saddle bag."

"They might catch us," she said.

"If they were going to give chase, they would have already caught us," he said. "Up ahead is a nice little grove of pinion where we can rest a little while and eat. Charity is exhausted, too, and so am I. It was a long night."

"Why'd you wait so long to come get us?" she asked.

"Thought I needed to wait until they were asleep. I didn't know Charity had laid the ground work for me to walk right in there like that and actually have help from one of them," he chuckled.

"Could you hear her?" Garnet asked.

"Yes, most of it. That dance she did around the fire raised hackles up my backbone. If I'd been an Indian, I'd have lit a shuck back to Chief Winnemucca and promised him my fidelity until death," he said.

167

He took Charity from her arms and laid her on the soft ground. By the time he turned to help Garnet she was already dismounted and untying the bedroll from the back of the saddle. She flipped it out with one deft movement and motioned for him to reposition Charity. The girl moaned when they laid her tangled red curls on the pillow, but she wiggled down into it as if she was in the best feather bed with the plumpest pillow in all of Nevada Territory.

Gabe scooped out a hole in the earth with his hands, edged it with rocks and filled it with limbs he found under the trees. Garnet watched him bring a small camping set from the saddle bags on her horse. A coffeepot, a pan to heat two cans of beans, a plate and one cup. They'd have to share the cup and plate, but she wasn't going to complain. For a cup of good, dark, strong coffee, she'd dance around that little fire herself.

Her gaze upon him made him nervous. She was alive. They were together and he had something to say but his tongue was stuck firmly to the roof of his mouth. His voice was as nonexistent as hers and his heart raced worse than it had when Imogene ran into the jail screaming about the Indians having taken Garnet and Charity. Uncle Zebediah had told him that the only thing that brought peace in his life was Aunt Nadine. He wondered if his uncle had to fight a legion of demons the day he asked Aunt Nadine to marry him?

Garnet waited impatiently, her mouth as dry as if she'd swabbed her mouth with cotton. The coffee had her full attention. One sip and she was sure she'd be able to go on to Frenchman's Ford without a grumble. When the aroma filled the whole campsite, Gabe deemed it done to perfection and poured the tin cup full, handing it to her first. For barely a second, she hesitated, not because she was being polite and about to let him have first rights to the cup of hot steaming coffee, but because in her weakened state, both emotional and physical, she didn't know if she could endure the shock of his touch on her fingers when she took it from him. Thirst won out over worry and she took the cup and gingerly sipped.

Heaven. Pure heaven, was that first mouth full. She had one more and then passed the cup to Gabe, who shut his eyes in appreciation. Coffee had never tasted so good. He gave the cup back to her and busied himself heating up beans over the fire. Charity sighed in her sleep and they both jumped, then got tickled because of their reaction.

"It's nerves," he said. "We'll all three be skittish for a while. Even if that Indian did give me his word he'd never come near Frenchman's Ford again, we'll be on edge. I bet Charity doesn't go wandering about after dark trying to conjure up ghosts for a long time."

"I bet Imogene never wants to go the river's edge for a picnic again," Garnet said.

"Just why did they leave Imogene?" Gabe asked, stirring the beans with the one spoon he carried.

Garnet blushed then got mad at herself. "Nature called. She was hid away in the brush taking care of it."

Gabe cleared his throat. "I see. Beans are hot. Shall we wake Charity or let her sleep?"

"Let her sleep. Never wake a sleeping baby," she said.

He dipped them up, scooted over next to her on the bare ground until their shoulders were touching, and took the first bite. While he chewed, he gave her the spoon and she filled her mouth. Almost as good as the coffee. Not quite. But almost. If she'd been able to think about beans rather than the fact she'd like to throw him down on the earth and kiss those inviting lips. She wouldn't even care if he tasted like coffee and beans all mixed up together.

Aunt Lulu told her once that sometimes a woman has to take things in her own hands because for all their bravado men folks were really just little boys inside. They were a bit stumble-bum about things of the heart and although they'd fight a grizzly with a switch from a hickory tree, they'd run a mile to keep from telling a lady how they felt. Somehow in the past years since Garnet had been making

her own way through the world, she'd been short changed
when it came to just how a woman went about taking things
in her own hands. Did she simply look at him in those
thunder filled blue eyes and tell him that she'd fallen in
love with him? Or did she, as propriety demanded, wait for
him to make the first call?

When the beans were half gone, she'd made up her mind.
She'd compromise. Just like she'd done with the sisters and
that mail-order bride's wagon train. She'd go along for a
spell to get to know the other Dulan girls, but she had no
intention of marrying someone she didn't know and surely
didn't love. This was the same in a different light. She'd
give him one week to step up to the plate and pick up the
bat. If he didn't, then she was going to tell him just how
she felt. If she'd been wrong about those long lazy looks
he kept shooting her way, and he said that all he'd wanted
was a bit of companionship, then at least she'd know and
could send him packing. If he returned the love she was
planning to hand him, then they could talk about the future.

What if his wandering days weren't over? What if he
wants to go home to Kentucky after a couple of years?
What if he wants to really go dig for gold in California?
Thoughts tumbled down from her mind to her heart so fast
she stopped breathing. Her heart put a stop to all of them,
when it simply reminded her that wherever he was would
be her piece of the promised land.

She smiled at that idea. The other sisters had found their
chunk of the promised land and she'd half-heartedly
scorned them when they mentioned it. Back in April, just
before they'd met at Jake's funeral, Willow, the last sister
to arrive, had crawled out of the stage coach at the Patee
House in Saint Joseph, Missouri. The hotel was enormous
and the look in Willow's eyes said that she'd been expecting something far smaller and not near so elaborate. The
driver had laughed at her and said that the hotel was full
that time of year with people waiting to get in their covered
wagons and go to California, to the promised land, he'd

said. Then he said, "They're all a bunch of fools because there ain't no promised land."

Willow had mentioned it when she wrote a letter to the other sisters from Nebraska where she stopped with Rafe. Velvet had found it in Wyoming; and Gypsy in Utah. Now if Garnet's heart was right, and she hoped so desperately that it was, her promised land would be in the middle of the desert in Nevada. Bless Gussie's heart, she was the only one left and real soon she'd be finishing the trip to California. Garnet hoped the man who drew her name was standing right in the middle of paradise, and that Gussie wouldn't have to endure a hanging, shunning and everything she'd faced to reach her own bit of heaven.

But that's the way of it. Even in the good book, they didn't get to enter into the promised land until they'd fought a good many battles, and the battles didn't stop at the border of the promised land, either, she reminded herself. *The fighting went right on as the people had to conquer lots more enemies.*

Garnet inhaled deeply, enjoying the brisk morning air. Fall had pushed summer back into the history books and winter was fast approaching. It didn't matter one whit to Garnet what season it was as long as she could have Gabe's love through them all. She'd fight whatever enemies there were for that love, because anything worth having was surely worth fighting for.

Go ahead and speak your mind, you lily-livered coward, Uncle Zeb's voice echoed in his ears, but he had a mouth full of beans. He'd do it the minute he swallowed because he couldn't stand the turmoil in his heart another minute.

"I bought Stella Nash's house on Friday. I started to tell you that night but we got off talking on something else," he said bluntly, trying to cover the fact that he intended to ask her if she'd like to live in it at the same time he told her about buying it.

"Oh?" Garnet said. "Why?"

"She came to me and offered it. She caught the eastbound stage on Saturday morning," he kept his eyes on the fire, afraid to look at Garnet. She'd refuse him, he figured. After all, she'd left the wagon train because she didn't want to get married.

"Why'd she make up her mind to do all that so fast?" Garnet asked.

"Oh, since the business with the seance, she's been a hermit. Wouldn't come out of the house because she didn't want to face the people. Her little temperance ladies pulled back and didn't even go to the Thursday night meeting. She's been thinking on the idea for a while now anyway, so she just up and walked across the street, all prim and proper and asked me if I wanted to buy her house," he said.

"And you did? Just like that?" Garnet asked, with a snap of the fingers.

"Yes, just like that," Gabe said, snapping his fingers back at her.

"Why?" Garnet asked.

"Oh, it's a good house. Her husband had it built well. I'm not a ranching or farming man, Garnet. I like living in town where I can keep my finger on the pulse of things. How about you? You a farm woman?" he asked, holding his breath.

"Sure I am," she said. "I love the farm."

His heart sank. Well, if that was the case, then he'd just have to sell Stella's house and buy a farm, some chickens and some cows, whatever Garnet wanted.

"I love the way you can have milk delivered from there, chickens brought in from there, not to mention fresh eggs, and vegetables," she laughed. "I lived with a cousin on the farm for a year when I was a little girl. Hated that year worse than any of my life. Got my hands dirty in the garden. I love flowers around the house and I'd plant a few vegetables if I needed to do so, but I'd rather buy them from the farm, which I love to visit once in a while, but I surely wouldn't want to live on one."

He laughed. "You had me going there for a minute."

"I know," she said. "To answer your question again. I'm not a farm woman. I love town. I love taking an evening stroll down the wood sidewalks. I like the people."

He looked up into her eyes, took her hands in his and leaned forward for a kiss, that literally sent sparks higher than the burning sticks in the fire. When he drew back the proposal was on the tip of his tongue, his heart sang a love song so pretty he wished he could form it into words. He opened his mouth to ask her to marry him, and a mop of red headed curls was suddenly between their faces.

"How long have I been asleep? Can I have the rest of those beans? I'm starving plumb to death. Can I have some coffee too? My mouth feels all nasty inside. But don't tell Momma you let me drink coffee. She says if you drink it before you're grown up that it will turn your toes all black. I couldn't ever catch a husband with black toes," she rambled.

Gabe handed her the plate of beans and poured up the last of the coffee. While she ate he rolled up the bedding and retied it to the back of his saddle. Was it fate that had just stepped in? Was he not supposed to marry Garnet Dulan?

"Man this is some good grub. We never did get any of that jerky last night, did we, Garnet? I haven't had a bite since those ginger cakes yesterday at supper time. Seems like that was a hundred years ago, don't it? How far are we from home? Reckon we'll be there by dinner. Land's sakes. This is Sunday. They'll be praying for us in church long about now," Charity said. "Either for our safe return or for the good Lord to receive our spirits unto Himself. I'm glad it's not our spirits because I reckon I've got some repenting to do the way I talked to the devil man. But then what else could I have done? They didn't trust in our God even if he is stronger than Lucifer. 'Course they don't know that. Well, that's all the beans and I'm still hungry but I betcha Momma has some chicken fried up. You both can stay for dinner. She'll fry aplenty in hopes that we come riding back in the yard all safe and sound."

"I think I just want a good, hot bath and a long sleep," Garnet said.

"To answer your question, we're about two hours from Frenchman's Ford," Gabe said.

Garnet wondered where that little bit of ice in his voice came from, and good grief was that thunder back in his eyes? What had brought that on? They were sharing the most intimate of looks and a kiss that was pure heaven just moments ago and now his face had a look that said he could do murder—and enjoy every moment of it.

Charity washed the dish and spoon with sand and handed it to Gabe. She kicked sand into the fire until it was extinguished and then declared that she was ready to go home. "And I don't ever intend to say that Frenchman's Ford is a boring place again. And if you ever see me out running down the road after dark again, Garnet, you just grab me and wail the tar out of my backside," she said.

"I might just do it," Garnet grinned as Gabe handed the child up to her.

"Oh, yes, I didn't mean to get in the way of your moonin' back there," she said loudly. "Someday I'm going to kiss a boy just like that, and get all starry-eyed like you two was. Someday when I grow up, but it sure ain't going to be Tommy Watkins."

Gabe burst out in a roar that shook his chest, echoed by a soft whisper giggle from Garnet. Their thoughts were the same. *Lord if we ever are blessed with children in our union, please give us boys. We couldn't handle a Charity in our home.*

Chapter Sixteen

Charity's brothers made a wild dash for the front door when they recognized the sheriff's horse and the other one with Garnet and Charity approaching. Charity began to yell and wave and Betsy and Matthew were on the porch long before the boys made it inside the house. They gathered Charity into their arms, tears streaming down their faces as they gave thanks for answered prayers. Matthew pulled a handkerchief from the back pocket of his Sunday trousers and blew his nose.

"Come in for dinner. It's ready but none of us could eat," Betsy smiled at Garnet.

"Thanks but no thanks," Garnet said. "I just want to go home and take a long bath. We ate a little on the trail, and I bet Thunder is thinking I've forsaken her."

"Gabe?" Matthew asked.

"No thanks. I'm going home and sleep all afternoon," he said.

"How can we thank you?" Matthew asked.

"No thanks necessary," Gabe said.

"They're both heroes," Charity said. "Why, Miss Garnet had them Indians scared out of their silly minds. She can only whisper and they thought she was some kind of ghost woman. Then here come Sheriff Walker and rescued us.

175

Left them Indians thinking we'd just flown away in the air. When they woke up, the probably wondered if they'd ever even run off with two redheaded girls, huh, Garnet?" Charity asked, winking from under her father's arm.

"That's right," Garnet said. "Charity has a long story to tell you I'm sure. But she was a very brave girl. Fought like a grizzly bear. Bit that one Indian on the hand and kicked the fire out of a few others before they let her ride on the horse with me," Garnet said. "So don't believe for a minute she didn't do her part."

A few minutes later they rode up to Garnet's porch. She slid off the horse's back with the notion that she'd just as soon never have to ride half a night followed by more than half a day again in her life. Gabe opened the front door for her and stepped in behind her.

"Garnet, I know you're tired and if you don't want to answer me right now, I'm willing to give you some time," he pulled her into his arms but left the door open so things would be proper should anyone be staring from behind the church.

"Gabe, I am tired. Can we talk tomorrow?" she asked, leaning down to pick up her black furry cat and hold it between them.

Gabe rubbed Thunder's fur. "Why'd you name her Thunder?" he asked, his heart heavy with words that needed to be said right then, not tomorrow.

"Because her eyes are the same color as yours," Garnet looked up to compare the two and sure enough they were. "And because the first time I looked into your eyes at the Silver Dollar they were filled with thunder. I had a notion to tell you that thunder is just a loud noise. It's the lightning that does the damage."

How true. Hers were filled with lightning and they'd sure enough done a work on his heart. He grinned and tipped her chin back with the back of his hand. Looking deep in those aqua-colored eyes, he found the other half of his soul and the kiss told him that what was on his mind wasn't going to wait another minute.

"Garnet Dulan, I want you to marry me," he said when they parted and he could breathe again.

"Why?" she asked.

"Because I want to live with you the rest of my life. Because I want to wake up every morning and see that red hair all fanned out on the pillow next to me. Because I want to sit in our parlor with you every night and tell you what happened that day. Because I want to go to sleep with you in my arms," he said.

"No, Gabe, I won't marry you for those reasons," she pulled back. "Now I'm going to take a long soaking bath, get all this grime off me and then I'm going to sleep all afternoon. Drop by this evening and we'll have coffee and cookies on the porch."

"Garnet, why?" he asked, thunder really filling his eyes.

"Because even though I want to wake up with you beside me, I can't marry you Gabe. Even though I want to spend the rest of my life with you. Even though I love you with my whole heart and being, I can't marry you," she said honestly.

"Why?"

"If you don't know then I'm not telling you," she said. "Now go away and let me have my bath and rest."

"But Garnet I love you so much. I don't understand," he said.

"Say it one more time," she whispered, an impish grin lighting up her tired face.

"What, that I love you? I do. I fell in love with you that first night I saw you. But I fought against it. Then when I found you layin' there under that tree. I thought you were dead, and I was so miserable. I love you and I've fought it and I'm tired of fighting it, Garnet," he said miserably.

"Yes, I will marry you. Tomorrow night at the Silver Dollar. My job will be to get things ready for the wedding.

Yours will be to talk Matthew into going into the saloon to marry us. Use the fact that he owes you and you're calling in the favor," she said.

"Why? Why did you change your mind?" He asked.

"My mind hasn't been changed," she kissed him again and wrapped her arms around his waist, her face on his chest, listening intently to the beating of his strong heart. "It's been the same for weeks. I've been in love with you, too. Not from that first night. I thought you were the most egotistical man I'd ever seen and I've seen a lot of big shot men. Not even from the time you took me to the undertaker. I don't know when it happened. Kind of gradual like, but it's happened all the same and my heart didn't change. It was just waiting for you to tell me you love me. Marriage ain't easy, Gabe. We'll have battles to fight and our lives to live. You have to love me for it to work, you see."

"Well, I do love you," he said, drawing her near for one more passionate kiss. "Now I'll drag in the tub for you and get on out of here," he said hoarsely, not wanting to let her out of the embrace. "You sure you don't want to be married in the church? Sure you don't want to wait a couple of weeks so you can make a white dress?

"I love you, too," she said. "Tomorrow is enough of an engagement for me. I'd like one of those plain wedding bands from Dusty's store. Nothing fancy. Just a plain one, now. Think you can get Matthew to the saloon?"

"Why there?" Gabe dreaded the ordeal of talking a preacher into performing a marriage in a saloon.

"Because it's where we met, and I think it will do the whole town, women included, good to go in there and see it's just a building. Lucifer doesn't live there," she said.

"No, Lucifer and his new wife are going to live down the street where the boarding house used to be. Think we'll ever fill up all those bedrooms?" he asked.

"We'll never know if you don't get out of here," she said. "Nine o'clock in the morning. That's when the ceremony will be. Tell the women folks to bring a covered dish and we'll have a pot luck brunch afterwards."

"I love you," he whispered once more just so she understood before he shut the door behind him and left her standing in the middle of the cabin.

"And I really do love you," she whispered behind his back.

Garnet dressed carefully in the first room she'd had when she lit in Frenchman's Ford. The room at the top of the stairs in the Silver Dollar. The bar maids flitted in and out offering advice, asking for help with their own hair and providing support. Betsy poked her head in at fifteen minutes before the appointed hour and gasped when she saw Garnet in her wedding finery.

"Well, now don't you look lovely," Garnet said.

Betsy wore her very best Sunday dress and the new hat they'd fashioned with satin roses and bits of lace. Her dress was a pristine navy blue with tiny buttons all the way from the bottom to the high neckline. A small bustle fluffed out the back where a big bow sat on her hips.

"It's a fact, I won't outshine the bride now, though isn't it," Betsy laughed and handed Garnet a bouquet she and Charity had made with flowers picked from Betsy's yard. They were tied with a big, wide white satin ribbon with long streamers. "Somehow I figured you'd be wearing white or maybe light blue."

"No thank you. Both of those colors make me look like a corpse," Garnet took the flowers and held them close. "Why, there's Mary Ann playing the wedding march. I guess it's time."

"Sure don't sound like when you play," Betsy said. "I've already detected a bunch of horribly sour notes."

"She's giving it her best," Garnet said. "I couldn't play and be the bride both. Just ain't possible. Is Gabe nervous?"

"Pacing. Been about to walk the shine off the floor for

an hour now. Jonah has had to make him sit down a dozen times. He keeps saying that you'll change your mind."

"Not me," she said. "Go on, now. I'll follow you down when you've taken your place in front of the bar."

"Me in front of a bar," Betsy laughed. "Things have sure changed since you come to town."

"Go," Garnet pushed her out the door.

Ruby Ann missed more than one note when Garnet appeared at the top of the stairs. The bride was beautiful, that was a fact. But dressed like that? It's a wonder Matthew and Betsy didn't walk right out of that saloon. Garnet wore the yellow dress trimmed in black lace that she'd borrowed from Emmy. It was still in beautiful shape, as was the head piece in her hair which flowed down her back to her waist. The hem of the dress, edged in lace, showed off black stockings and the tops of her shoes, with just a touch of slim ankles visible when the skirt tail swayed from one side to the other.

Gabe could hardly believe the vision when he looked up from the bottom of the stairs and saw his future bride in a bar maid's dress. It was a good thing Stella Nash had left town. She would have dropped on the floor in a pure fit of apoplexy. But to Gabe, his bride was the most beautiful woman in the world, even with that scar around her neck and the raspy whisper of her voice. He'd fallen in love with her the first time he saw her in that yellow dress, and now she'd borrowed it to wear for him again.

She was glad he'd left off the suit coat and worn his black trousers, a black leather vest and string tie with his best white shirt. She was equally as glad he'd chosen to wear his badge, because that was exactly the way he looked the first time she saw him. Except there was no thunder in those blue eyes today. At the bottom of the stairs, she slipped her arm in his and together the two of them crossed the floor to the bar where Jonah waited on one side, serving as best man, and Betsy, as matron-of-honor waited on the other.

Matthew performed the ceremony. The women, barmaids and saints alike, served a lovely brunch and by ten o'clock everyone had gone home.

"Shall we?" Matthew offered her his arm.

"Wait just a minute," Garnet said, picking up a small package, wrapped in brown paper from Dusty's store and tied with a bit of ribbon like the one around her bouquet. "Imogene and Charity said we were to open this together when we got home this morning."

He nodded, and the two of them strolled down Main Street.

The sheriff and the barmaid.

Mr. and Mrs. Gabriel Walker.

When they reached the door of the boarding house, he picked her up and carried her over the threshold, setting her down at the bottom of the stairs long enough to kiss her soundly, one more time. He kicked the door shut with the heel of his boot. Tomorrow he'd go to work. Today was their honeymoon.

"Oh, my!" she exclaimed. "Did you buy the furniture, too?"

"Yes, and everything else. She just packed her own personal belongings. You can change whatever you want. As long as you don't change your mind about us," he said.

"I will. I don't think the sheriff should live in a house with pink trim. And I won't change my mind. Not ever," she said. "Now let's open this present."

She untied the ribbon the paper fell away to reveal a heavy piece of paper, with ribbon and lace trim; a long piece of twine attached to each end with the words, *Do Not Disturb* written in a little girls flourishing handwriting.

They both giggled at the sign. Garnet marched over to the door, pulled back the curtain covering a glass window over the top half and set in the window but it immediately fell to the floor.

"Here, let me," Gabe said, unpinning the badge from his

vest. Using the silver star he affixed the sign to the curtain and left it there for the whole town to see.

"Signed by the good sheriff of Frenchman's Ford, and anyone who enters faces the thunder in his eyes," she giggled in that low voice he'd come to love.

"Worse yet, anyone who knocks on this door today faces the wrath of the lightning in the eyes of the good sheriff's wife. I love you, Garnet Walker," he said, removing the head piece from her hair and running his hands through all that glorious thickness.

"And I love you Gabriel Walker. Forever," she looped her arms around his neck and brought his mouth down to meet hers. The promised land. She'd found it right there in Northern Nevada Territory. Right there in Gabe Walker's arms. Best of all, in his heart, where they would forever share the promised land, no matter where the journey might lead them.

Westville Public Library
Westville, IL 61883